MW00479953

SHIELD MAIDEN

SHIELD MAIDEN

THE LONE VALKYRIE™ BOOK 1

CHARLEY CASE   MARTHA CARR   MICHAEL ANDERLE

This book is a work of fiction. All of the characters, organizations, and events portrayed in this novel are either products of the author's imagination or are used fictitiously. Sometimes both.

Copyright © 2020 LMBPN Publishing
Cover by Fantasy Book Design
A Michael Anderle Production

LMBPN Publishing supports the right to free expression and the value of copyright. The purpose of copyright is to encourage writers and artists to produce the creative works that enrich our culture.

The distribution of this book without permission is a theft of the author's intellectual property. If you would like permission to use material from the book (other than for review purposes), please contact support@lmbpn.com. Thank you for your support of the author's rights.

LMBPN Publishing
PMB 196, 2540 South Maryland Pkwy
Las Vegas, NV 89109

First US edition, March 2020
Version 1.04, May 2020
eBook ISBN: 978-1-64202-793-8
Print ISBN: 978-1-64202-794-5

The Terranavis Universe (and what happens within / characters / situations / worlds) are Copyright (c) 2019-2020 by Martha Carr and LMBPN Publishing.

DEDICATIONS

From Charley

This book is dedicated to my wife and best friend, Kelly.
Without her belief in my abilities, and patience to see the
process through, this book wouldn't exist.

From Martha

To all those who love to read, and like a good puzzle inside
a good story
To Michael Anderle for his generosity
to all his fellow authors
To Louie and Jackie
And in memory of my big sister,
Dr. Diana Deane Carr
who first taught me about magic, Star Trek,
DC Comics and flaming cherries jubilee

From Michael

To Family, Friends and
Those Who Love
To Read.
May We All Enjoy Grace
To Live The Life We Are
Called.

CHAPTER ONE

Heather Resnick crouched beside the thick trunk of an old Western red cedar, seeking a reprieve from the persistent nighttime rain. The boughs of the ancient sentinel, heavy with water, drooped low but held off most of the late-spring shower.

She adjusted the two long daggers at her waist before pulling the hair tie from her ponytail and angrily regathered the stray hairs that had fallen into her face over the last hour-and-a-half trek through the forest. Quickly spinning the long black hair into a tight bun, she re-secured it with the tie and wiped the rain from her eyes.

"Why am I the one sent out into the middle of the woods every time? Victoria knows I hate the woods," Heather mumbled, checking her watch. A vine around the base of the cedar seemed to droop at her words. Heather sighed and stroked the young plant tenderly. "Not you, little one. I love you. I'm just grumpy is all. I know you don't understand this, but my underwear is soaked from this fucking rain, and my socks feel like sponges left in

1

dirty dishwater. I would kill for a mission that took me to a beach somewhere. Hell, at this point, I would kill for a dry pair of underwear."

The vine seemed to be satisfied with Heather's answer and pushed itself into her stroking finger like a cat trying to get every ounce of love it could from the simple action. Heather smiled and stroked the vine a few more times.

As a Valkyrie, Heather's nature affinity was with vines and grasses, and she was able to call for their assistance when needed. Compared to some of her sisters, like Victoria, who could communicate with crows, or Mindy, who had entire wolf packs at her beck and call, Heather's nature affinity was mild. She *could* use it in very interesting ways, but it had taken her nearly a thousand years and twenty lives to get there.

Checking the small full-color display of her watch again, Heather zoomed the tiny map out to get her bearings. She had to zoom out again before the map showed anything with a name attached to it.

The town of Elk River was a good five miles to the south through wild forest. Ironically, there was no Elk River, as in a body of water. There *was* an Elk Creek, although anyone who's seen a river and a creek would know the difference, but she supposed she would let the little town have a pass. It wasn't like they had much else going for them, being out in the middle of nowhere in Northern Idaho.

She sighed, switching the small screen off and peering into the dark woods around her. The constant patter of fat raindrops drowned out most of the forest sounds, but frogs and crickets trying to continue the species by attracting mates made a sort of buzzing undercurrent of noise that further confused her senses.

"How the fuck am I supposed to find some dark magic user if the forest won't shut up for one minute?" she grumbled. "Dammit, Victoria! How about next time you give me a little more than 'Oh, we think there's a bad person out there using dark magic. Go find them and deal with it.'" She ground her teeth. "*You* go deal with it, sister, if it's such a big problem."

"You do like to talk, don't you?" a voice that sounded far too much like a young girl's to be out in the woods alone in the middle of the night said behind Heather.

The Valkyrie spun around, her hands now holding the two long silver daggers in a defensive pose.

A slightly built but obviously adult woman in a hooded black robe stood not three feet away. Her face was obscured by the dark hood, but the wet robe clung to her form. Arms crossed, she reminded Heather of a mean girl from high school. She was unarmed.

The five towering half-wolf, half-human forms in a semicircle around her, on the other hand, were the definition of living weapons. Their wolf-like heads had teeth bared and ears laid back, ready to pounce. Long taloned fingers flexed, and their thick black tails swayed in the breeze.

Unlike werewolves, these creatures didn't seem to have intelligence behind their yellow eyes beyond that of a dog, just a powerful lust to chase Heather down and maul her to death.

The hooded woman saw Heather staring at the eight-foot-tall beasts with wide eyes. "You like my Rougarou?

3

They were a gift from my master," she said, a smile in her girlish voice as she reached over and petted one of their furry arms. "They're not very smart, but they are loyal."

Heather blinked and stood up straight, her initial shock wearing off. She was a good six inches taller than the black-robed woman. The initial fear fell away when she saw that there were only six of them, and five were just big dogs. This fight was going to barely warm Heather up before it was over.

Her face fell to a thin-lipped frown. "You're the one causing all the trouble out here? I'll have you know I've been traipsing through these woods looking for you for the last hour and a half, and I hate being out here. Now I'm pissed off. Come on, you goth reject, let's get this over with so I can get home and have a hot cup of tea and get out of these fucking soggy clothes."

The woman threw back her hood, revealing the face of a woman in her early thirties with wavy blonde hair. She giggled, putting a hand to her lips. That was very childlike and creeped Heather right out.

"I'm Seline," she said coyly. "What's your name?"

Heather raised her daggers and readied herself. "I am Heather Resnick, Valkyrie of the Sisterhood, and the last person you will ever see."

Seline's eyes went wide, and Heather saw that they were mad. "Oh, a Valkyrie! Master will be so pleased to have you as a pet. I'm glad you came to see us."

"I didn't come to see you, idiot. I came to kill you. Now, tell me where your master is, and we can get this over with," Heather growled, gripping her daggers tighter.

"Oh, don't worry about that. I'll take you to him soon enough," Seline said in a deep and ominous voice.

The Rougarou all attacked at once, five sets of talons coming at Heather with astonishing speed.

Heather put her arm up almost casually and formed a protective shield that wrapped halfway around her in a bubble. The talons raked against the invisible shield sending out sparks that glowed golden in the night.

Bunching her legs, Heather sprang forward, using the shield to bat the Rougarou off their feet and onto their backs, getting within striking distance of her target. Her freehand pointing the silver dagger at the robed figure's heart as she thrust.

The smile was back on Seline's face as she held out a hand to intercept the incoming shield. "So strong! You'll be a great snack!"

A black mist poured from Seline's fingers, slamming into the shield and coating its surface like a viscous oil. Heather had anticipated something like this, but dark magic usually had a hefty tinge of red to it. This spell was blacker than the night that surrounded them.

Rougarou were regaining their feet, heads shaking in anger and frustration. One let out a howl that was quickly picked up by the other four. Then the forest filled with the sound of howling wolves. There were dozens of return calls, most close by, and all of them had a tinge of pain to their timbre.

A sharp pain in Heather's blocking arm made her suck breath through her teeth. She saw that the mist had eaten a hole in her shield and was now pouring onto her arm, eating through her leather coat sleeve. She redoubled her

5

efforts and poured celestial magic into the shield, and the hole closed up, but to her horror, the mist was acting like acid on her magic.

"That's not possible," Heather said through gritted teeth.

"It's been a while for you, hasn't it?" Seline giggled. "You all thought infernal magic had passed from this world, didn't you? Silly Valkyries." Her girlish features darkened as she leaned in and lowered her voice to a harsh whisper. "Your time on this ship is over."

The infernal magic flowing from Seline doubled, then tripled. Heather struggled to keep up, channeling everything she had into her shield. With mounting dread, she realized it wouldn't be enough. Her shield was thinning despite her best efforts, and a quick glance around showed that dozens more of the Rougarou had shown up after the call had gone out, surrounding the two magic users, waiting for their opportunity to strike.

Heather knew this was going to be the last few minutes of her body's life. She would be back, but it would be another twenty years before she remembered she was a Valkyrie. She needed to let her sisters know what was happening up here.

Dropping her dagger, Heather reached up to her watch and quickly scrolled to a button she had never used before. She hesitated, not wanting to be wrong, but when her shield suddenly formed several holes and infernal magic began to burn its way into her, she jabbed the button.

The watch, attached to her magically enhanced phone, sent a warning out into the aether.

Two thousand miles away, Victoria Gara's phone

chimed with a pre-written text that all Valkyrie-issued phones had stored in them.

Sitting in her board meeting at the head of the long wooden table, Victoria picked up her phone and read the text she always dreaded to see. One of her sisters was dead.

"I'm sorry, Thomas. I need to take this. Can we reconvene in an hour?" Victoria interrupted the man speaking.

Thomas stuttered to a halt. "Of course, ma'am."

Victoria stood, adjusted her gray pencil skirt, and walked out of the meeting, her heels cracking across the marble floor like angry gunfire.

CHAPTER TWO

Victoria appeared in the never-ending white nothingness of Elsewhere, the place between life and death where a Valkyrie did their most important work. She was the first to arrive as usual and summoned up a large blue felt wingback chair from nothing.

Sitting carefully and crossing her legs in the pencil skirt took more grace than most would think, but Victoria made it look as natural as breathing. Working in the upper echelons of the business world for the last hundred years had taught her how to maneuver in restrictive business attire with ease.

She opened her attaché case and began going over the notes from the board meeting earlier that day.

"Always work with you, sister," a girlish voice with a thick Southern California accent said, making Victoria look up.

A young woman she had never seen before stood with her hands on her hips; two bouncy, blue-dyed pigtails brushed her shoulders. She wore a plaid miniskirt and thigh-high black leather platform boots that were laced all the way up the front and added five inches to her short frame. She wore a cropped long-sleeve t-shirt with *Wagner is my Spirit Animal* written across the stretched fabric holding her ample chest at bay.

While Victoria didn't recognize the body, she did recognize the person.

"Hello, elder sister," Victoria said with a smile as she put the attaché case on a side table that materialized out of nothing as she let go of it. She stood and embraced the young woman. "I was hoping you would return to us soon. Since your last death, things have been a little hectic." She pulled back and took the woman in, brushing her fingers through one of the blue pigtails. "I see this body is going through its rebellious phase. What are you, sixteen?"

The woman laughed. "Fifteen. God, I was a little shit right up until the moment my memories came back. It happened a day and a half ago, and I've been putting out fires ever since."

"I hate waking up as an asshole," Victoria agreed. "It's so much work to get back on track. What is this body called?"

"Missy Walker," she said, rolling her eyes. "God, even my name makes me sound like a brat. That's what you get for having parents born and raised in SoCal."

Victoria shrugged and chuckled. "I always found SoCal to be great. The weather was nice, and people seemed adventurous."

Missy rolled her eyes. "The last time you spent any time there was during the Gold Rush, Vicky. It's changed a little since then."

Victoria laughed. "That's true. What can I say, Sweden called to me. I love it here."

Missy summoned a chair of her own, and the two women made themselves comfortable while they waited for their sisters to arrive.

"I'm glad you're back," Victoria said with a relieved sigh. "I don't know how you handle all the sisterhood business so easily. Every time you die, I have the worst decade and a half of my current life."

"Practice," Missy said, crossing her leg over her pale knee, the heavy platform boot pulling her foot down at an extreme angle so her calves touched on the outsides. "I'm several thousand years older than you. I was my last sisterhood's eldest too. Speaking of that, is there anything I need to be up to speed on before the others arrive?"

Victoria's smile faded. "Yes. Heather sent out her distress call. She was investigating a large patch of corruption in Northern Idaho. We think it's a dark magic user who's set up shop. Unfortunate, but part of the life cycle. I was going to send Gretchen out to see what happened, but now you get to decide who to send," she said with a wry smile.

"Have we lost anyone else?" Missy had dropped the affectations of her young body and was all business.

"No, we're all still here, though a couple have had to use the Reaper and are now Lone Valkyries. They are still in communication, but it'll be a few more years until we can get close." Victoria smiled. "That brings us to the most interesting thing that's happened since we first took passage on Earth: there's a new Valkyrie."

Missy's eyes went wide. "A new Valkyrie? How is that even possible?"

"I have no idea. Her name is Mila Winters. She's an anthropologist at the Denver Museum of Nature and Science. Smart, pretty, and has a singular will that is impressive, to say the least."

"Well, I can't wait to meet her."

Victoria laughed. "It'll be a while until that happens. She's already used the Reaper; second day I met her, too. It was quite impressive to watch. She cut the darkness out of a witch so far gone I didn't know it was possible to do."

Missy considered that. "Interesting. I assume you gave her one of our phones and are instructing her from afar?"

"As best I can, but my help really isn't required beyond the occasional question. Turns out she's not only the first new Valkyrie on Earth, but she's also the champion of a hero. A dwarf who showed up out of nowhere she calls Finn. He's teaching her combat and magic."

Missy smiled. "A champion. Well, that *is* good news. I need to see what she's capable of as soon as possible. I think I have an idea about that."

She was cut off as Valkyries began appearing all around them. It was time to get back into the swing of things.

"Hello, sisters. It's good to be home."

CHAPTER THREE

D r. Mila Winters sat cross-legged in the center of the large blue mat that padded the dojo in her fourth-floor condo, wearing a maroon sports bra and matching leggings. Her long black hair was up in a ponytail to keep it from sticking to her post-workout sweat-slick back.

Eyes closed, she was attempting to meditate, but her boyfriend, Finnegan Dragonbender, was sitting opposite her doing the same. He was driving her nuts.

She loved the six-five dwarf with everything she had, but he was one of the loudest quiet people on the planet. His even, meditative breathing sounded like a train struggling to get moving, with huge sucking intakes and whooshing exhales.

Mila cracked an eye and smiled when she saw the look of raw determination on Finn's face. His cheeks were clenched so tight that his thick full beard shook.

Only Finn would think that meditation could be achieved through sheer grit.

The huge dwarf sat in the same cross-legged position with their legs nearly touching, each of them with hands resting on knees. Unlike Mila's relaxed hand position, Finn's were clenched in fists that matched his furrowed brow.

Penny perched on the back of the couch, watching with amusement as Finn struggled to maintain the practice.

She had met Finn and Penny, a foot-and-a-half-long blue faerie dragon and Finn's constant companion, less than a year ago during a chance encounter at a Kum & Go on the outskirts of Denver. His ship had crash-landed in the mountains, stranding him and Penny on Earth.

Over the next few months, she had learned a great deal about the planet she called home, such as that Earth wasn't a planet at all, but a huge ship that was supposed to be transporting people and goods across the galaxy. It had become stranded in the sun's gravity well thousands of years ago, and everyone on the planet was a descendant of the original passengers.

To top it all off, every one of those passengers had been magical in nature, even the humans, though the rest of the universe called them Peabrains due to the pea-sized section of their brains that allowed them to channel magic. That didn't mean that everyone nowadays had magic—just the opposite. Some event had occurred thousands of years ago that led to every Peabrain forgetting about magic, turning them into the "normal" people who populated most of the globe.

At first Mila had been excited that she might be one of the few Peabrains to "awaken" and be able to access her magic. Over their months together, they realized she was not going to awaken because she had already done so as a Valkyrie. Not just another Valkyrie, but as a new Valkyrie, something that hadn't happened in all the millennia Earth had been circling the sun.

A creaking sound emanated from Finn's right arm as he tried to clench his prosthetic hand tighter.

From Finn's shoulder down, he had a dwarven prosthetic replacing the arm he had lost in their last major battle. A witch that had been consumed with dark magic had withered the appendage to the point that even healers or powerful potions couldn't return it to functionality.

The prosthetic was connected to him magically and responded like a normal arm with smooth movements and precise control, but at the cost of a constant trickle of Finn's magical stores. The latticework of diamond-like material called "impact diamond" mimicked the shape of his previous arm perfectly, with the exception that there were large gaps between the material like you would see on a trellis. The whole thing looked like a piece of art, with its ribbons of yellow diamond material glinting in the light, but Mila knew he could crush steel with it if he wanted too.

"Babe." Mila sighed, putting a small hand on his fist. "You need to relax. That's the whole point of this kind of meditation."

Finn's eyes popped open, and he stared at her for a few breaths before unclenching his body. Mila hadn't realized how tense he had been until she saw his shoulders drop a full three inches.

"I almost had it," he grumbled.

Mila snorted a laugh. "Hardly. You looked as tense as a

pig at a sausage factory. It's fine. Obviously, this kind of meditation isn't for you. I have a feeling you might be better at the movement meditations. We know you can do battle meditation."

He smiled and nodded. "I do tend to get into the zone when I'm swinging Fragar. Nothing clears the mind like a good fight."

Finn stood in a fluid motion that spoke of his athletic prowess and held out a meaty hand to Mila.

She took the offered hand and was pulled up to her full height, which was more than a foot and a half shorter than Finn's six-five. Mila liked to think that what she lacked in size, she made up for in smarts. Her magical gun helped as well.

"I can't believe you're still wearing those," Danica said, eying Finn's black leggings as she came around the corner with a steaming Cup of Noodles in her artificial hand.

The tall blonde elf was their roommate and Mila's best friend. Like Finn, she had lost her hand fighting the Dark Star while protecting Mila. Unlike Finn, her prosthetic was only from the forearm down, but it was made of the same material and of the same intricate design as Finn's. Mila once again considered the implications that two of the people she loved had literally given their right arm to protect her, and her heart swelled at the thought of having such loyal and strong people around her.

Mila and Danica had moved in together years ago when they were both in school, Mila going for her Ph.D. in anthropology and Danica her MD at the University of Colorado. Although they'd both entered the workforce, they'd never moved out on their own and had been like sisters ever since.

Danica smiled as she leaned her butt on the back of the couch beside Penny and shoveled a forkful of ramen into her mouth.

Finn glanced down at the form-fitting pants Danica had bought him as a joke for complaining that it was the only thing she and Mila ever wore.

He looked up and smiled, nodding toward the black leggings Danica currently wore. "What can I say? I get it now. They're perfect for working out, and my legs look amazing in them." He popped a hip at Danica that made her snort noodles out her nose.

After a short coughing fit, she held out a hand. "Oh, my God. You have to warn a girl before doing that. I almost choked to death."

Mila chuckled and headed for the kitchen, but slapped Finn's ass on the way. "I can't say I mind. You want some pancakes?"

"Shir shee!" Penny trumpeted, sitting up with wide eyes.

Mila gave the small dragon a set of finger guns and winked. "I wasn't even going to ask you, Penny. I assume you *always* want pancakes."

"Chi?" she asked, looking around at the others for confirmation.

Mila laughed. "Yeah, you're that predictable. Anyone else?"

Finn nodded, and Danica looked down at her noodles. "Now that half of these were in my nose, I'll take a stack of pancakes instead," Danica said, giving the Styrofoam container a look of disgust and following Mila to the kitchen, where she dumped it in the trash.

"Chi shir!" Penny lamented.

"Ew, gross!" Mila said, pulling the flour out of the cupboard. "Why would you want to eat those? She literally shot them out of her nose."

Penny stood on her back legs and gave Mila the sassiest head weave she had ever seen. "Shir shee shee," she said in a mocking falsetto.

Mila's mouth dropped open. "I am not too good for leftovers! There is a huge difference between leftovers and snotty ramen."

Finn rumbled a laugh. "I've seen her eat a rat."

Danica shrugged, skirting around Mila, who was cracking eggs in a bowl, and opened the fridge, pulling out three bottles of iced coffee. "That's not so bad. I've had squirrel before. That's sort of like a rat."

Finn shook his head, taking a seat at the kitchen's island counter. "You don't understand. It was a live rat, and it was eating Bunto droppings at the time. No matter how smart she is, I couldn't get her to understand that if the rat ate the turds, *she* was eating the turds," Finn said, taking one of the bottles Danica offered to him.

Danica gave Penny a sidelong glance, using her diamond-hard hand to pop the top off Mila's iced coffee before setting it down. "Is that true? You ate turds?"

Penny rolled her eyes, hopping off the couch and flapping her wings a few times as she swooped over to land on the counter beside Finn. "Squee shir chi."

Mila measured a spoonful of vanilla into the mixing

bowl and frowned. "I mean, I get that you gotta do what you gotta do, but it's a turd, man. That's nasty."

Penny shrugged before crawling into the empty fruit basket and using it as a lounge chair.

Finn gave her a level stare. "That was hardly a 'do what you gotta do' situation. We were coming out of a restaurant after a victory meal. Remember? We had just finished with that Androg dungeon system when we re-appropriated the Hestar Idol. You ate that turd rat because you wanted to."

"Okay," Danica said, holding up a hand to stop the conversation, "we really need to stop talking about this. I want to enjoy my pancakes, not think about eating turds. Let's move on, shall we?"

"Good point," Mila said, using a whisk to mix the ingredients. "Danica, can you turn on the griddle to warm it up?"

"Sure. I'm going to cut up some fruit too. You guys want some?"

Everyone nodded, and Mila leaned a hip on the counter as she beat the batter. She gave Penny a discerning look. "How are you doing, Penny? We've all settled in pretty well together and have our projects. Finn has his work helping the magical community, and I'm still learning about my powers from Victoria. What do you have going on lately? I feel like ever since the battle with the Dark Star, you've been a little quiet."

Finn raised his eyebrows and looked at the little dragon. Even Danica turned to regard her over Mila's shoulder.

Penny raised an eye ridge and looked at each of them in

turn before deflating. She clasped her fingers over her belly and began to twiddle her thumb talons, obviously reluctant to talk about whatever was on her mind.

"You okay?" Finn asked, suddenly concerned that he had missed something his friend was dealing with.

Penny gave a nod but didn't look at them. "Shir squee shee. Chi chi," she said quietly.

Finn and Mila's eyes went wide and they both froze. Danica, not being versed in draconic, glanced at the three of them for a translation, frustration etched into her sharp elvish features.

"Well? What did she say?" she finally burst out.

Mila's mouth began working before Finn's. She opened and closed it a few times, still staring at Penny before getting some traction. "She said she needs to lay her eggs, and that it's time for Finn to help her gather her hoard."

Finn and Penny had been together for decades, but the reason they'd worked together in the first place was due to a promise they had made to one another. She would help him in his treasure hunting business if, when the time came, he would help her gather a hoard. Faerie dragons were special in that there were certain conditions a hoard required to work for them, which was why there are so few of them in the galaxy. Up until now, Penny wouldn't tell Finn what those stipulations were, always that it would come later. It seemed that later was about to be now.

Danica's mouth made an O and her eyes grew large. "Is this what you were talking about when the two of us were at Preston's cabin?"

Penny nodded.

Danica quickly skirted the island and sat on the stool

beside Finn, her attention on the dragon. "Okay, girl. Spill the beans. I want to see some baby dragons."

Penny glanced up at the excited face of her friend and smiled. Obviously encouraged by Danica's glee, she sucked in a breath and began to explain.

CHAPTER FOUR

Forty-five minutes later, they all sat rubbing full bellies while Penny belatedly shoveled her pancakes in her mouth, having not eaten while she explained the whole process to them. Finn had translated for Danica. Penny had talked nonstop for longer than any of them had heard her do before. Now that she was done, she ate ravenously, only stopping to pour more syrup on each layer of fluffy cake as she got to it.

"Let me try and sum this up," Finn said, opening a second bottle of iced coffee and taking a sip before returning to his stool. "You needed a family surrounding you to start producing eggs, which the three of us fulfill."

"Chi shir," Penny corrected, around a mouthful.

"Right, sorry. You needed people who considered *themselves* your family surrounding you to start producing eggs."

Penny nodded, and Danica gave her a sappy, misty-eyed smile while pressing her hand to her chest. The move made

Penny roll her eyes, but she did sneak a wink at Danica when no one else could see.

"And now you need me to go out and steal treasure that has cultural significance and bring it back here for you." Finn sighed. "But I can't just give it to you, you have to 'steal' it from me, even if I know you're doing it?"

Penny nodded, a ring of smoke tooting from her nostril.

"No wonder there are so few of your kind," Mila said, shaking her head. "From a cultural viewpoint, this is a very convoluted process to have a baby."

Penny gave her a knowing look and nodded.

"Well, there's a problem," Finn said with a frown. "I'm not going to go steal the crown jewels from England or something, so how am I going to get this done?"

"Would treasures from the past work? Like, sunken treasure?" Danica chimed in.

Penny shrugged, then nodded.

"Oh." Finn waved a hand. "Okay, I can do that. Lost treasure is my bread and butter. What are some of the most famous lost treasures here on Earth?"

Mila laughed. "Are you serious? You're just going to go out there and find lost treasures? No mess, no fuss? They're called lost treasures because no one can find them."

Finn shrugged. "I'm a dwarf," he stated as if that explained everything.

Mila gave an exasperated smile. "What does that have to do with anything? The treasures are still lost."

He leaned an elbow on the island counter and turned to

her, a white-toothed smile peeking through his full brown beard. "I can smell it."

Her shoulders slumped in a 'this is ridiculous' manner. "You can smell it?"

He nodded. "Yup. Well, sort of. I can sense it." He waggled a hand at chest height. "Kinda. Back me up here, Penny."

The tiny dragon begrudgingly nodded, licking syrup from her muzzle. "Chi shir."

"Really?" Mila didn't know what else to say.

"Really. How do you think me and Penny sto...recovered all those artifacts before we met you?" He put a finger to his nose and gave her a wink. "The nose knows."

"Shir," Penny amended, stuffing another bite of breakfast in her mouth.

Finn nodded in agreement. "Yeah. Sort of. It's not really a sense of smell kinda thing."

"What *is* it, a sense of kinda thing?" Danica asked, lounging back on her stool and putting her feet up on Mila's lap as she took a drink of her iced coffee.

The position Danica ended up in took considerable balance and grace. Mila knew if she ever tried to lounge like that while sitting in one of the low-backed stools, she would end up on the floor.

Mila unconsciously reached down and affectionately began to rub the top of Danica's sock-covered foot. "Yeah. If it's not smell, then what is it?"

Finn squinted and looked off into the distance while he tried to put words to the feeling. "I guess I can just feel it in my bones."

"That's convenient for a treasure hunter." Mila chuckled.

"Why do you think I started hunting for treasure? I work hard, but I also work smart." He winked. "So, Miss Anthropologist, what are some of the juicy treasures out there waiting to be found?"

Mila looked at the ceiling as she continued to stroke the top of Danica's foot. "Let me go grab one of my books. I might have a few ideas."

Danica lifted her feet as Mila slid off the stool and headed for her and Finn's room. "Good. Now that Penny's done eating, we can move this to the couch," the tall blonde elf said, finishing the iced coffee and tossing the bottle across the room and into the recycling bin with a crash.

Penny licked the last bit of syrup up from the plate before leaping onto Danica's shoulder. The two of them went to the large L-shaped couch, and Penny hopped onto one of the back cushions as Danica flopped into a reclining position along the short side of the L. Finn joined her, taking his normal position at the other armrest as Mila came out of the bedroom, a large coffee table book with a picture of the Sphinx on the cover open as she scanned through the glossary.

Without taking her eyes from the book, Mila circled the couch and plopped down right where Danica's legs would have been if the elf didn't have the reflexes of a cat and quickly pull her knees to her chest. As soon as Mila was seated, Danica stretched back out, draping her legs over her friend's lap.

"What do you have for me?" Finn asked.

Mila started chuckling. "Well, there's the Ark of the Covenant. That's probably the most famous lost treasure."

Finn nodded. "Okay, sounds good to me. Where is it? In general, that is. Obviously, you don't know exactly where it is."

Mila shrugged, turning to a particular page in the book. "Nobody knows. Probably in the Middle East, but some people think it might be in England or Scotland. There's not a whole lot known about it once it was stolen."

"That's a lot of ground to cover," Danica said, her brows rising. "Some people think it's in Scotland? Why?"

"There's a theory that the Lost Tribe of Dan might have taken it there," Mila said as she read a passage in the book.

"Yeah, that might be a little too much ground to cover," Finn said, now a little less confident. "What else do you have?"

Mila read a little more before her face lit up and she began talking to herself. "That's right. I couldn't remember if they found it."

"Found what?" Danica asked, craning her neck to see what Mila was reading.

"The treasure of Montezuma the Second," Mila said, finally looking up from the book as she rested it on Danica's shins. "At the end of the sixteenth century, Cortés and his men sacked the Aztec capital Tenochtitlan and murdered the emperor, Montezuma the Second. The city went nuts, attacking the conquistadors and driving them out of the city. The Spanish weren't going to get away weighed down by all the treasure, so they dumped the gold into Lake Texcoco. Over the years, people searched for it but found nothing. After a while, the lake was drained as the Spanish began settling the area, but they never found the gold."

"Where is Lake Texcoco? I feel like I've heard of it before?" Danica asked, a narrow-eyed look of half-recognition on her face.

"It's the lake that used to be where Mexico City now stands. And that's the really interesting part. Back in 1986, they were doing some construction on a museum on Avenida Hidalgo and they dug up one of the gold bars. They didn't find any more, but they now know Cortés did dump the gold."

Finn sat up, his face full of excitement. "Perfect! I don't even have to hike to some mountain or go looking at the bottom of the ocean. I can handle a city, no problem. Shit, I can probably get this done by dinnertime." He jogged off to his and Mila's room, leaving the rest of them sitting with open mouths.

"There is no way he can find that treasure by dinner time," Mila said, shaking her head. "There's, like, seven hundred years of city built over the site. Do you have any idea how many times Mexico City has been rebuilt?"

"Chi. Squee shir," Penny said matter-of-factly.

"Oh, I don't doubt his abilities as a treasure hunter," Mila said, then cocked her head to the side in consideration. "Actually, I don't have a frame of reference for how good he is. I've never seen him do a treasure hunt. I mean, the whole hellhound thing was like a treasure hunt, and that only took a day or two." After a second, she shook her head emphatically. "There is no way. If he comes home with a sack of gold tonight, I'll... I don't know. I'll do something I hate."

Danica smiled evilly. "You could go for a ride with him on his motorcycle. We all know how much you love that."

Mila felt her face go white. The idea of being on a motorcycle with Finn driving scared the shit out of her. She would never admit it out loud, but the thought of not being in control while on a motorcycle made her palms sweat.

Ever since Finn had gotten his Triumph, Mila had found excuses not to ride with him. She had used the fact that it was too cold for about as long as she could, but now with spring nearly over, she was going to have to come up with something new.

"Oh, that is evil," Mila growled at her now-laughing friend. "You know I hate the idea of riding on that thing."

"You hate the idea of not controlling that thing," Danica shot back, laughing harder when she saw the look of guilty shock on Mila's face. "That's it. That's the bet. If he comes back with the gold tonight, you owe him a ride."

"Fine, but if he doesn't come back with the gold tonight, you have to do all the laundry for a week," Mila countered.

Danica closed her mouth, and her face went serious. She hated doing laundry with a passion. She glanced at Penny, who gave her a subtle nod. "You really think he can find the treasure in a day?" she asked the dragon.

A single smoke ring puffed from her nostril in answer.

"Deal!" Danica shouted, taking Mila's hand and shaking it before she could back out.

"Hey, wait a minute! I didn't know Penny was so sure," Mila complained, but she knew she was caught, and her shoulders slumped. "Fine. It's a deal. There is no way he does it by dinner."

"Does what by dinner?" Finn asked, coming out of the bedroom wearing his "adventuring" gear: a black t-shirt and jeans with a brown leather harness that went over his shoulders and held a few healing potions, along with his axe Fragar.

The axe was a dwarven-made weapon that folded down into itself until only the handle remained. He had given Mila two items that were similar: a shirt of mythril chain-mail that she was now bonded with, and the sword Gram. The sword folded down impossibly when stored like Fragar, but the armor had bonded with her and was now a part of her, coming out when she said the word of power that activated it.

"Find the treasure," Danica said. "We have a bet going."

Finn's brow went up. "Oh?"

"You don't get to know the details. This is between just us girls," Mila quickly added, not wanting him to know that she bet against him.

He smiled. "Okay, keep your secrets. Danica, can you teleport me down to Mexico City? I want to get moving."

Danica rolled off the couch and onto her feet. "Sure. I always like teleporting."

Finn held out a hand and pulled Mila up. "I'll be back soon."

Mila put her arms around his neck and stepped up onto the couch so they were closer in height. "You be careful. How will you get back?"

He shrugged, a big smile on his face. "I'll find someone local. Maybe I'll call Hermin or Garret. Don't worry about it."

She smiled at his excitement. "You really missed this, didn't you?"

"Yeah, I think I did. Plus, who doesn't want to see some dragon babies?"

Mila laughed. "That *will* be pretty special." She nuzzled his neck, squeezing him tight for a second before pulling back and kissing him deeply. "Be careful."

"You already said that," he teased.

"I mean it. I love you."

"Love you too."

"Chi shee shee," Penny said with an eye roll, pretending to shove a taloned finger down her throat.

"*You* get a room!" Mila shot her a dirty look.

Penny held up her hands in surrender. "Chi."

Finn laughed. "Look after her while I'm gone," he said over Mila's shoulder to the snickering dragon.

Penny gave him a thumbs-up.

"Okay, let's go," Finn said, stepping close to Danica.

Without a word, Danica held her hands out, and a bubble formed around the two of them. It popped and they were gone, only the faint smell of roses lingering in the air.

CHAPTER FIVE

Mila folded her legs and fell into a cross-legged position on the couch as soon as Finn and Danica left. Penny reached out and patted her head. She crawled down from the back of the couch into Mila's lap.

They stared at one another in the sudden silence of an empty house. Finn might be loud, but she had come to be comfortable in his chaos.

"You want to watch a movie?" Mila suggested with a questioning shrug.

Penny's eyes filled with panic. "Shir shee."

"No need to worry about that." Mila chuckled, picking up the remote from the side table. "We are definitely *not* watching a John Wayne movie."

Penny sagged in relief, then situated herself so she was sitting in Mila's lap while using her stomach as a backrest.

Mila's phone rang, and she handed the remote to Penny as she pulled her phone from the thigh pocket of her leggings and checked the caller ID. Preston Meriwether's name flashed on the screen.

Preston was the de facto governor of the magical community for most of the western United States and happened to be one of the richest men in the world. Mila and Finn had done quite a bit of work for him over the last year, but it still boggled her mind to get the occasional call from such a famous figure. He was also one of the few Minotaurs left on *Earth*.

Quickly hitting the accept button, she put the phone to her ear. "Hello?"

"Dr. Winters, so good to hear your voice." Preston's mellow baritone floated out of the phone. "How have you been?"

"Pretty good. I've had quite a few interesting conversations with Victoria about my Valkyrie." She chuckled. "How has the reconstruction been going?"

Preston's manor on the south side of Denver had been leveled in the battle with the Dark Star. She knew the construction was dragging since he was a public figure and couldn't use obvious magical construction methods with the media closely watching the progress.

"Slow, but it's coming together. It was a blessing in disguise, really. The grounds and house needed an update anyway. Mind you, there were a few artifacts I would have liked to save, but in the end, insurance is covering most of the cost of the rebuild, so I can't complain too much."

"Not that money is a problem," Mila said, then turned red with embarrassment when she realized what she had said.

Preston laughed it off. "That's true. I am extending the underground bunker, though, so a lot of that cost is falling to me. The staff and I were packed in pretty tight during the battle. I want to make sure I have enough space for my people next time, just in case we have to stay down there for an extended period."

Mila was grateful he didn't take offense, but now she was nervous she was going to say something else stupid and figured getting down to business was the best move. "Good plan on building more bunker space. I assume you didn't call to chat. Is there something I can do for you, Preston?"

His rumbling chuckle made her phone vibrate against her ear. "Actually, there is something I was hoping you and Finn could check out for me."

"Finn is out of town, but Penny and I could help."

He was silent for a few seconds as he considered. It was just long enough that Mila felt a little insulted that Preston thought she couldn't handle whatever it was without Finn. Then she thought about some of the things she and Finn had done for Preston and agreed it might be a little too much for her. He answered before her mind spiraled out of control.

"I suppose you two would be a better choice than sending Finn anyway. He does tend to...make things happen."

Mila laughed. "Yeah, he is a one-man natural disaster sometimes."

Preston snorted, his large nostrils perfect for the emote. "That's just a fact. He's a good man, but a little straightforward at times."

"Tell me about it. He thinks he's going to find Montezuma's gold before dinner tonight." She laughed.

There was a moment of quiet contemplation from

Preston. "You know, if anyone could do it, it would be Finn."

Mila rolled her eyes. "Not you too! Am I the only one who thinks finding a lost treasure should take more than a day's work?"

"Well, he *is* a dwarf. They're kind of built for this kind of thing," Preston said matter-of-factly. "Luckily, I don't need you to find any lost treasure.

"There is an elvish settlement in northern Idaho that supplies the Trinish Mushrooms we use in medicine at the Menagerie. Anita let me know that they missed their last delivery, and she hasn't been able to get hold of anyone at the settlement. Luckily none of the magical beasts are ill, and we have a small stock of the mushrooms, but it's odd that we haven't heard from them. I was hoping you could head up there and check in with them. I would send a G.A.E.L. team, but the elves there are a little nervous about the strike teams."

Mila's eyebrows rose as the story went on. "You don't seem all that concerned. Have they lost touch before?"

"Well, yes." Preston laughed. "The settlement is pretty free with the mind-altering drugs. A few times in the past, they have gone offline for a week or so while they searched their inner minds in a drug-induced haze. Nothing dangerous, but they usually let me know before they do it. I didn't hear anything this time, and I just want to be sure they're okay."

Mila could appreciate that Preston wanted to be sure the people in his area were doing fine, and she didn't have any plans for the rest of the day. "Hey, Penny. Want to go up to Idaho and check on some hippy elves?"

Penny tilted her head up until she was looking at Mila upside down, the top of her head wedged between Mila's breasts. She considered, then nodded, hitting the power button on the TV, not having found anything to watch anyway.

"We're in. Where is this settlement?" Mila said to Preston.

"It's just outside a tiny town called Elk River. If you go to the town, then head northeast, you'll find them pretty easily. You can also ask around town. I know they do their shopping in Elk River and are known by the townsfolk."

"Okay, sounds good. I'll give you a call later and let you know what I find."

"Thank you. I look forward to talking to you later," Preston said, a smile in his voice.

"Talk to you later." Mila hung up and slid the phone back into her pocket. "I guess we're heading into the woods. I could use a good walk. We can have Danica take us up when she gets back."

Penny nodded, launching herself into the air from Mila's lap. She flapped her way toward her room to get ready.

Mila got up, deciding a sports bra and leggings were not the best choice to meet townsfolk in northern Idaho, and headed for her room to change.

Rummaging through her closet, she decided to keep the leggings and added a form-fitting ribbed green sweater and a thin denim jacket to hide the back of her corset holster. She was tying her hiking boots when her phone began to ring again.

Pulling the phone from her pocket, she was confused to

see that the screen was dark. Then she heard another ring and realized it was the phone Victoria had given her a few months ago. The phone was magical but only worked when contacting people in the sisterhood. Mila frowned as she went to her bedside table and pulled the phone out of the drawer. She had scheduled a call with Victoria for later that week, so getting a call early concerned her.

"Hello?" Mila said tentatively.

"Mila." Victoria's deeply feminine voice oozed out of the earpiece. "How are you, dear?"

"I'm doing fine. Is everything okay? I thought our call was scheduled for later this week?" Mila sat on the edge of the bed and began lacing up her second boot.

"That's what I'm calling about. I'm stepping down as leader of the sisterhood. Our eldest has rejoined us, having turned fifteen in her new body."

"Oh, I didn't realize you weren't the eldest." Mila sat up, her eyes wide. "Will you and I not be working together anymore?"

No, no. Nothing like that," Victoria reassured her, "but Missy wants to speak to you during our call on Friday. But before that, she wants to see what you've learned during our little chats and what your Finnegan has been teaching you."

"Uh…" Mila raised an eyebrow as she headed back out into the living room. "I thought as a Lone Valkyrie, I can't get near other Valkyries without sapping their power. It's kind of the whole reason we've never met in person."

Mila smelled a sudden rush of roses and glanced toward the dojo just in time to see Danica pop back into the condo. Her mouth was open in shock as she met Mila's eye. Mila gave her a questioning look but pointed at the phone to let her know it would be a minute.

"That's true. We can't meet for long before my powers would be drained, but Missy has a mission for you," Victoria explained.

"A mission? That seems a little out of the blue. Shouldn't I get a lot more training or something? I don't even know all the rules of the sisterhood." Mila leaned her butt on the back of the couch and crossed her arm over her chest.

Danica walked to the fridge and cracked open a beer, chugging half of it with a thousand-yard stare.

"The rules are pretty easy," Victoria said with a sigh. "We follow the lead of the eldest sister, help the magical community as best we can, and do our best to keep from being discovered as Valkyries. We took passage on this ship to hide from infernals in the first place, so that just makes sense. That's about it."

"Okay, so, what? I do this mission, then we talk about it on the phone?"

"Pretty much." Victoria chuckled. "She's heard all about you from me, but I think she wants to get a feel for you herself. Feel free to take Finn with you. You two are a team, after all."

Mila sighed. "You're the second person today to mention that they wanted Finn to go along. He's down in Mexico for the day or longer. I'm betting longer."

"Shir shee chi!" Penny said, swooping out of the small door to her room.

"Penny thinks he'll be back by this afternoon, but I have my doubts," Mila added, rolling her eyes at Penny.

"That's actually better as far as an assessment goes," Victoria said, adjusting the phone as the sound of shuffling paperwork came through the line. "One of our sisters has gone dark, and is more than likely dead. She was tracking down a spot of corruption that showed up on our radar. Lisa had reports from a small town in northern Idaho that the wildlife was acting peculiar, a good sign that there is dark magic about. You have experience with dark magic, so you know what to expect."

"Heather didn't?" Mila asked, shocked that Victoria was so nonchalant about the possible death of a sister.

"Unfortunately, Heather hadn't had to deal with any dark magic users for some time." She mumbled to herself for a few seconds. "Shit. She hadn't had to deal with it for well over a hundred and fifty years. Anyway, she was never that good of a fighter. If she died, we can use it as an excuse to get her back into training."

"That seems kind of cold, Victoria. This is a woman's life we're talking about. One of our sisters." Mila was horrified.

"Not exactly." Victoria sighed as if having to explain the same thing to a child for the hundredth time. "If she did die, she'll be back in a few decades. That is what it means to be a Valkyrie. There is very little in the universe that can truly kill us, and we vanquished the last of it on Earth thousands of years ago. I know this is your first life and these things must seem a little odd to you, but trust me. Sometimes a good death is all you need to get your life back on track."

Mila shook her head in wonder. "I'll have to trust you on that one. So, what is it Missy wants me to do?" Danica had finished the beer and opened another, and Mila began to worry.

"We just want you to go check it out. If it's more than you can handle, give me a call, and the sisterhood can come take care of it. It's a pretty isolated place, so we don't have to hurry, but the sooner, the better. Do you know anything about northern Idaho?"

"My father's from there. Lives in Sandpoint with my mom, almost at the Canadian border. Why? Wait, northern Idaho? Don't tell me it's near Elk River."

There was a moment of silence on the other line. "How did you know?"

Mila bit her lip, a sudden feeling of dread coming over her. "Preston Meriwether asked me to go check on an elvish settlement there. Said the people have been out of contact for a while."

"Hmm." Victoria considered this new development. "I don't like this. Maybe I'll head up there myself. We can tell Missy it was too dangerous and send you out on the next one."

"No, it's fine. I'm heading up there anyway to check on the elves. If I'm just doing some scouting, it shouldn't be too big a deal. Besides, I don't want to be the first time I meet our eldest sister to be after I was too chickenshit to go on a mission she sent me on. I'll be careful. Plus, I'll have Penny with me."

"Chi?" Penny asked, her eyes wide.

Mila gave her a dirty look before sticking her tongue out at the dragon. "I'll call you when I find anything out."

"Okay. I'll email you a picture and what info we have on Heather. Maybe she's not dead and just badly hurt." Victoria's tone softened, and she leaned into her microphone as if she didn't want others around to hear her. "Be careful. I haven't met you in the real world, but I would like to before you get a new body."

Mila chuckled. "Thanks for the vote of confidence. I'll talk to you soon." She hung up and tossed the phone on the couch as she turned to face Danica, who was almost done with her second beer. "What the hell happened? Why are you freaking out? Is Finn okay?" she asked as a shock of fear for the big dwarf came over her.

Danica turned to her slowly, her thousand-yard stare still in place. "He's fine. I just teleported us into a strip club. In the early morning. In Mexico City. It was...intense."

Mila started laughing. "Why would you teleport into a strip club?"

Danica blinked a few times and did a full-body shiver. "Well, I've never been to Mexico City, so I didn't have a particular place in mind when I activated the spell. But just before that, I was thinking that I don't know many girls from Mexico except you, but you're half Mexican and grew up in the States. Then I thought about Maria Gonzalez from undergrad."

Mila cocked her head to the side as she tried to place the name. Her eyes lit up when it came to her. "The girl in our Trig classes? Didn't she become an engineer or something?"

Danica nodded. "Aerospace engineer. She builds rockets for one of Preston's companies, I think."

"What does that have to do with you teleporting into a strip club in Mexico City?"

Danica swallowed. "How do you think Maria paid for college? Here's a hint: she didn't take out any loans."

Mila's eyes went wide. "She was a dancer? How do you know that?"

"She asked me if I wanted to dance when I was having money troubles during my sophomore year."

"So, you were thinking about strip clubs when you activated the spell."

Danica nodded.

"Okay, but you've been to a strip club before. Why the shell shock?"

"Let's just say this particular club got pretty inventive to draw in clientele at 8am on a Monday."

Mila started laughing. "How did Finn take it?"

Danica frowned. "He took one look, said it was about as good as a Talurrian Dancing show, and walked out."

Penny grasped her chest and let out an "*Eep!*"

Mila saw Penny's face flush purple. "That bad?"

Penny shook her head slowly.

Mila's brows went up. "That good?"

A single ring of smoke shot from Penny's flushed nostril.

CHAPTER SIX

W hen Mila filled Danica in on the two phone calls leading her to Elk River, Idaho and said she and Penny needed a teleport up there, Danica told her she was coming with her. She needed to be outside in nature to unsee what she had witnessed.

Mila was grateful to have someone to watch her back since Penny did more watching the front, a trait she had picked up from Finn, who always charged into situations headfirst.

After looking up the town on the internet and finding a surprising number of photos, they picked a spot behind what looked like a bar. After collecting their gear and passing out the in-ear communicators, Danica cast a concealment spell on her bow and quiver since they didn't fold down like Mila's sword Gram and teleported them behind the only bar in Elk River.

One second they were standing in their condo, and the next, the smell of dumpster and roses filled Mila's nose, sending her into a coughing fit.

"Oh, man," she wheezed between coughs. "I did not expect to get a lung full of garbage smell teleporting out into the wilderness."

Penny snickered and launched herself off Mila's shoulder to fly over to the dumpster and take a look inside. "Shir shee."

"Yeah, rotting pub food wouldn't be all that appetizing," Mila said, stepping away from the back of the building to get away from the smell of hot garbage. "Careful, Penny. There's a huge yellowjacket nest above you, and they don't like that you're so close." She pointed to the nest in the corner where the roof met the wall.

Penny looked up and shrugged. "Chi chi, shee."

Mila laughed. "I suppose they would have to be pretty badass to get through dragon scales. I didn't think about that." She looked around to get a better assessment of where they had ended up.

They were in a town of sorts. The back of the bar had a gravel lot that was empty at this early hour, but beyond the edge of the gravel was grass field for a hundred feet, then nothing but forest. She could see several mountain peaks in the distance, snow still clinging to the tops even in late spring. Mila was surprised that there was only the main drag and two side streets to the whole "downtown" area of Elk River. A single row of buildings lined each side of the main drag, and beyond that, it was basically wilderness in all directions.

"That's so weird," Danica said, cocking her head.

"What?" Mila turned in a slow circle but didn't see anything.

"It's so quiet."

Mila hadn't considered how quiet it was, mostly because the coughing fit had set the blood to thudding in her ears. Now that Danica pointed it out, Mila was surprised that there was nothing but the rustling of trees and the occasional animal sound.

"Whoa." Mila nodded, a smile on her face. "That's kinda nice. I've lived in Denver for so long I don't even hear the city anymore, but now that it's not there, it's kinda spooky."

"Chi chi," Penny said, holding up a finger.

Mila listened, and after a few seconds, did hear the sound of an engine getting closer. "You should probably stay out of sight, Penny. I don't know how people around here might react to you."

Penny nodded and flew back over, landing on Mila's back and crawling under her jean jacket, leaving a notice-able lump near her waist.

"That's not what I meant," Mila said, opening one side of the jacket to reveal Penny's face. "I'm not big enough to hide you."

"Chi shir," she said, pointing to the side of the building where the parking lot let out onto the main road.

Mila dropped the jacket and glanced up just in time to see a jacked-up truck pull into the gravel lot. A thirty-something man in a red plaid shirt and a baseball cap had an arm out the window and gave them hard look as he parked at the back of the lot—far from the smelly dumpster, Mila noted.

Mila decided it was time to get this investigation

started and approached as the man climbed down out of the truck.

"Excuse me," Mila began with a smile as she pulled her phone out of her pocket and opened the email with Heather's picture in it. "Have you seen this woman? She's a friend of mine, and we haven't heard from her in a while."

The man raised an eyebrow, looking Mila, then Danica, over from head to toe before clearing his throat and glancing at the photo.

"Might have." He sniffed. "Who are you guys? Under-cover cops?"

Mila chuckled. "Do we look like cops?"

"Well, if you're undercover, you do. You're obviously city folks, and I'm thinking you don't know this woman all that well. Makes me think you're cops." He adjusted his cap and looked down at Mila with an unflinching sureness.

Mila swallowed. "What makes you think I don't know her?"

The corner of his mouth went up in a half-grin. "Because you're not freaking out. If your good friend was lost in the woods and you had to come up here to find her, I expect you'd be pretty frantic. But you two are cool as a cucumber salad. Makes a guy wonder." He glanced around the empty parking lot. "Where's your car? Long way from Boise to not have a car."

"We're not from Boise," Danica corrected with a little more force than Mila thought necessary.

"What's wrong with Boise?" Mila said, looking over her shoulder at Danica.

The elf shrugged. "Nothing. We're just not from there."

"I'll have you know I spent many weekends in Boise growing up. It's a pretty cool city." Mila frowned.

Danica held her hands up in surrender. "I'm not saying there's anything bad about Boise. I'm sure it's wonderful, but it's no Denver."

"So, y'all are from Denver, then?" the man asked with a smile.

Mila turned back to him, her face red with embarrassment. "Yes. We are from Denver. Look, we're not cops, undercover or otherwise. This is a...work associate who's gone missing, and I was sent to find her, or find out what happened to her. Do you think you could help a girl out?"

The man gave her a long appraising look, sucking his teeth and glancing around as if to see if there was anyone within earshot. "Tell you what, I'll answer your questions if you answer mine first. I just have two."

Mila nodded, not seeing what it could hurt. If she didn't like the questions, she was sure she could find someone else in this tiny town who wouldn't make them jump through hoops. "Okay, deal."

"First question: who do you work for?"

Mila made a pained face as she thought about how to explain her situation. "I don't work for anyone. Well, technically, I work for the Denver Museum of Science and Nature, but I'm on sabbatical, so right now, I guess you could say I'm freelance."

The man raised an eyebrow considering her answer. "Okay, but someone sent you. Was it Meriwether?"

Mila's eyes went wide at the mention of Preston.

He cracked a smile. "Okay, now we're getting somewhere. My second question is this: what are you?"

"Excuse me?" Mila blurted, caught off-guard, still reeling from the Meriwether comment.

"Well, your tall and rather attractive friend over there is an elf, and I'm pretty sure you have a baby wyvern under your jacket. Either that or you have a tail," he said, pointing his chin at her waist.

Mila glanced down and saw that Penny's tail was hanging out from under the hem of her jean jacket. As she watched, the tail was slowly retracted and a muffled, apologetic "Chi" could be heard coming from her back.

With a mighty sigh, Mila looked up into the smiling face of the good ol' boy as he smugly adjusted his cap again. He had them and was obviously a magical in his own right. She decided she needed to figure out how to spot magicals when they were using concealment spells in the future.

"I'm a Peabrain," Mila said, unable to admit the truth.

He sniffed again. "No, you're not, but that's okay. You're close enough, whatever you are. You don't know much about this town, do you?"

"Not particularly. Should I?" Mila asked.

"I guess not." He spread his arms in a wide arc that took in the whole town. "This is Elk River, one of the few towns that is completely populated by magicals. I'm Harvey, Elk River's mayor and one of only two bartenders." He held out a hand for Mila to shake.

She took the offered hand. "Mila Winters. It's nice to meet you, Harvey. I had no idea there were towns that were only for magicals."

He shrugged, reaching out to shake Danica's hand. "It happens. Hi, I'm Harvey."

"Danica," she said, shaking the offered hand.

"To answer your questions, yes, I saw your friend two nights ago. She was chatting up a lady at the bar until about ten o'clock, then left. Haven't seen her since," Harvey said, closing his truck's door and stuffing the keys in his tight jeans' pocket.

"Chatting up, like hitting on her?" Mila asked.

Harvey chuckled. "It seemed like it, but she was god-awful at it. I think she was trying to get info out of her."

"Who was the lady she was talking to? Did you know her?" Danica asked.

Harvey nodded. "Yeah, she's new in town. Been here a few weeks, but I only met her twice before that night. I think her name's Selina, or maybe Seline; I can't remember. Anyway, she bought the old logging camp north of town, and supposedly is going to turn it into a camp or something."

"That's at least a start," Mila said, biting her lip, not sure how much she wanted to involve this guy. "What about a settlement of elves outside of town? Do you know anything about them?"

"Sure, bunch of hippies even for elves, no offense," he said with a tip of his hat at Danica, who just snorted a laugh. "They keep to themselves. Come into town every once in a while, but I haven't seen 'em for a few weeks now. Mind you, that's not unusual for them."

"Where is their camp?"

"Is that why Meriwether sent you up here? Did something happen to them?" Harvey asked suspiciously.

Mila gave a shrug. "Not sure. That's why he wants me to go check it out."

Harvey nodded. "They're good folks, so I hope they're all right. Yeah, their place is about ten miles up the main road, then there's a dirt road with the sharp left that goes up the mountain. They're about two miles up into the woods." He looked around the parking lot again. "I'm guessing you teleported up here and don't have a car. Do either of you know how to drive a bike?"

"Like a bicycle?" Mila asked hopefully.

He chuckled. "Like a dirt bike. I have one here I'll lend you, but you gotta promise to bring it back in one piece."

"I don't know how to drive a bike," Mila admitted. "I mean, I do, but not very well."

"I do," Danica said with a smile.

Mila gave her a disbelieving look. "I've never seen you drive a motorcycle."

Danica smirked at her. "You know I did had a life before I met you, right?"

"We met freshman year of undergrad. We were basically still kids."

"Elves are 'kids' for a long time. I did a lot of things before college."

Harvey gave her an appraising look. "Tall, beautiful, a college girl, and knows how to ride a motorcycle? Where have you been all my life, darlin'?"

"Easy, cowboy, she has a boyfriend," Mila said, dryly. "Besides, she would spend you out of house and home with her leggings budget alone."

"Are you saying I'm high maintenance?" Danica asked, her mouth hanging open in mock offense.

Mila put her hand on Danica's shoulder and gave her a

serious look as if breaking bad news to her. "Danica, we're in the middle of Idaho, about to ride into the woods on a dirt bike, and you put on eyeliner before we left the condo."

Danica stuck her nose into the air. "There's no reason we can't look good while kicking ass."

CHAPTER SEVEN

"This is my nightmare," Mila shouted over the wind and the buzzing of the dirt bike's engine.

When the only response was Danica's shoulders shaking with mirth, Mila gritted her teeth and tightened her grip around the elf's torso.

Harvey didn't have any helmets to go with the bike, which made Mila nervous, but Danica assured her she could protect the both of them if they crashed. So now Mila was feeling the full force of sixty-mile-an-hour wind in her face, and she had to occasionally spit out Danica's long hair that got stuck in her mouth when it was blown back.

Mila glanced at Penny with jealousy as she kept pace with the bike, wishing she could do the same just so she didn't have to be on the death machine. Danica was having far too much fun, taking turns faster than Mila thought prudent.

Penny glanced over and gave Mila a thumbs-up and a

big grin. Mila just stared at her with a dark look she hoped said everything she was feeling.

"I think this is the road Harvey was talking about," Danica shouted with her head turned slightly and pointing at the upcoming dirt road with one hand.

Danica only had one hand on the handlebars, which made Mila want to scream, but she nodded instead, not wanting to sound like a wimp.

Danica took the turn fast enough that they skidded a few feet when they hit the gravel, eliciting a squeak of fear form Mila. Danica expertly drifted the bike and laid on the gas. They shot up the gravel road, spraying rocks and dust behind them in a rooster tail.

The bow slung over Danica's shoulders was pressed between them hurt Mila's right breast, but she squeezed tighter, screwing her eyes closed and accepting that she would have a bruised tit for a day or two. She would take a bruised chest over falling off the back of the bike any day.

Two minutes later, the engine's whine finally let up, and Danica slowed to a stop before shutting the bike down.

"We're here," Danica said, patting Mila's hands, which were still clamped around her torso. "Babe, you can let go. That was a fun ride, wasn't it?"

"I hate you," Mila said, slowly opening her eyes and letting go of Danica.

Danica laughed and put the kickstand down, tilting the bike to the side and eliciting another squeak of fear form Mila, making Danica laugh all the harder.

"I really hate you." Mila laughed, swinging her leg over the back of the bike and fighting to not fall to the ground and kiss it.

Danica parked the bike a good hundred feet from the end of the road. Several old vehicles were parked along the lane and in the grass where the road widened into a rough turnaround at the end of the gravel road.

Danica adjusted her bow. "Dude, I think I'm going to have a bow-stave-shaped mark on my back for a week."

"It'll match my tit," Mila said, rubbing her now-throbbing chest.

"What?"

"Nothing," Mila grumbled, scanning the area.

Penny had flown into the camp proper and was circling above the clearing in the woods, scouting the area as Mila and Danica made their way up the last hundred feet of the road and squeezed between an old Ford pickup and a Subaru that was more rust than metal.

Mila could see several simple wooden buildings, all of them facing the center of the clearing. Approaching from the back, it looked like they could use a coat of paint.

The smell of wood smoke suddenly hit Mila's nose as they came closer to the clearing.

Glancing at Penny while she followed Danica, Mila saw the tiny dragon hovering over the center of the settlement turning in a slow circle, her mouth open in shock.

"I don't think anyone's home," Danica said cautiously as she unslung her bow. "What the hell happened here?"

Mila looked out into the clearing as they passed the first building and saw what Danica meant.

The settlement had obviously been a lively place to live, with a large area in the center of the clearing where dedicated to bonfires and a small stage erected to one side for performances or musical acts. Each of the little houses was individually decorated with lively paint schemes and hand-made furniture on the front porches. It looked like a place where people felt comfortable being themselves and reveled in the community they had created.

It also looked like a tornado had ripped through the settlement. Trash and broken furniture littered the common area. The bonfire had obviously gotten out of control at some point and left a large blackened area in the grass, along with the closest house, which had burned down to a blackened pile of ash. Most of the homes had their doors swinging open in the slight breeze, or torn off completely.

"Holy hell," Mila muttered. "It looks like they were dragged from their homes. Look at the furrows in the ground. People digging in their heels as they were pulled into the woods. Look," she pointed across the clearing where the woods thickened into a wall of foliage, "they took them that way."

She pulled out her Ivar pistol and checked that the safety was off before spotting her dragon friend still hovering thirty feet up. "Penny! You see the drag marks?"

Penny nodded, pointing off into the forest. "Shir."

"Can you follow them? Don't get into any trouble, but see if you can find out where they went."

Penny nodded and shot off into the trees like a blue streak of lightning.

"We should check the houses to be sure no one is in need of healing," Danica said.

"Once a doctor, always a doctor, huh?"

Danica turned to her with a confused look on her face. "I'm still a doctor."

"That's what I said," Mila argued, scanning the houses before moving toward the closest one. Its door had been torn from the frame and was stuck in the soft ground corner-first like it had been thrown with great force.

"You said, 'once a doctor always a doctor.' That's what you say when someone used to be a doctor, but they still try to help people," Danica responded quietly, drawing an arrow from her quiver and notching it with practiced ease.

They had been friends so long that they knew the senseless conversation would make the other feel better while in a stressful situation. Conversation was their love language.

"Right, sorry," Mila apologized with little conviction. "I guess I meant to say that you're a doctor, so of course you would want to find survivors."

Mila led the way up the steps onto the porch, her pistol out in front of her as she approached the eerily quiet home's entrance.

"It's all good. Just didn't want you to think I had quit the hospital and wouldn't be able to pay the rent," Danica said stoically, staying on the grass and drawing back the arrow, covering the entrance as Mila approached.

Mila quickly turned and pressed her back against the exterior beside the opening like she had seen any number of TV cops do. After a few quick breaths, she leaned over and took a quick look inside to be sure there wasn't anyone waiting in the dark.

She didn't see anything, so she stepped into the one-room house, the Ivar still at the ready. It had a surprisingly spacious interior, considering the small structure. A couch and a small wood-burning stove occupied the front room, with a tiny kitchen and dinner table under a loft. The loft held a queen-sized bed and had a thin staircase leading to it, and its underside served as a bookshelf along one wall.

There was no sign of anyone, and after a few seconds of no sound but the wind, Mila determined the place was empty. That didn't mean it was peaceful inside.

The entire place had been ransacked, either in a robbery or during a struggle. Books had been pulled from the shelves, plates had been smashed on the floor, and the table was broken in half from something large landing on it.

"See anything?" Danica called from behind Mila.

"Nothing. The place was destroyed, but there's no one here. We should check the rest of the houses," Mila said, squinting at the arm of the couch. It had been sliced open several times with what looked like a razor-sharp knife, all the way down to the wooden frame.

They moved on to the next house, and it was the same story—the house empty and torn to shit. This one had several of the same cuts in furniture, and the rug had been sliced nearly in half.

In the third house, she finally understood what she was looking at.

"Danica, come here," Mila said from the open door, waving for the tall elf to come inside.

When they were both standing in the front room, Mila pointed at a wingback chair that was sliced to shit. "What does that look like to you?"

Danica raised an eyebrow at the ribbons of fabric that used to be a comfortable chair. "Uh, it looks like someone went hog-wild on a chair with a knife or a sword or something."

"Yeah, that's what I thought at first too," Mila said, stepping closer to the chair and leaning over, making sure Danica could see what she was doing. "Every time something is cut, it's been completely shredded. At first I thought it was just some psycho chopping away, but I think whoever did this was covering up what we're looking at."

She held out her hand like she had claws, her fingers spread as far as they would go and began to trace the lines cut into the fabric. It was hard to see at first because there were so many cuts, but once she showed Danica the pattern, Mila heard a gasp from her friend.

"Oh, my God. Those are claw marks?"

Mila nodded. "I think so, but I've never seen claws this sharp. Usually there would be more of a tearing patten, but these cuts are super-precise. It's almost like they were wearing gloves with razors in the fingertips."

"Or there's a magical element to their claws," Danica said, fingering one of the cuts. "Let's check the rest before Penny gets back. I don't want to accidentally leave anyone behind."

Mila nodded and stepped out onto the porch. Movement from her right side made her hackles rise, and on pure instinct, she dropped to a knee as a branch slammed into the doorframe inches over her head.

Mila's eyes refused to understand what she was seeing.

A woman who had at one time been an elf if her pointed ears and almond eyes were any indication stood on the porch brandishing a three-inch-thick tree branch as a club. The woman's face was twisted in a snarl reminiscent of a dog with rabies. Foam spurted from between clenched teeth, and her red eyes ran with bloody tears. The most disturbing part about her was that large portions of her dirty and naked body were deformed and far too large for her frame, as if she had been half turned into an eight-foot-tall body-builder. If that weren't bad enough, all the disfigured portions were covered in a thick, wiry black and gray fur.

She snarled, lifting the branch over her head to strike again, but Mila, seeing her opening, launched her shoulder into the exposed stomach of the deformed woman. Her momentum drove them across the small porch and over the railing in a tumbling ball.

The woman screamed in rage and fury, bringing the branch down on Mila's back as they fell.

With a whispered word of power, Mila's mythril armor rose from her body in a fine chain mesh that covered her from neck to waist under her clothes, and the branch slammed into her and exploded into splinters.

The chainmail absorbed most of the impact, but Mila's back still protested with shooting pain. Knowing that the mythril could stop a bullet with minimal pain, Mila was shocked at how strong the woman had to be to hit her with a tree branch that hard.

They slammed to the ground, Mila driving her knees into the woman's stomach while pushing herself up into a kneeling position and aiming the pistol at her face.

"Freeze! I don't want to—" Mila was forced to put her arm up to block the incoming fists as the once-elf went berserk.

Mila felt her powers activate just the way she had been

practicing, and a half-circle of power formed instantly as a shield in front of her. She mentally attached the shield to her forearm, then let go of the power, anchoring the invisible barrier to herself so she didn't have to focus on it anymore.

The incoming fists slammed into the invisible barrier, causing the shield's surface to ripple with golden light at the impact sites. Mila was nearly thrown back from the force of the blows, but she quickly planted a leg behind her on solid ground while keeping a knee on her attacker's chest and leaned into the ferocious attacks.

Mila could see the vacant look in her attacker's eyes. Whoever this woman used to be, she wasn't in there anymore. This was just a beast that needed to kill.

Danica landed beside the two of them, a nocked arrow pointed at the thing's head. "You okay?"

"Yeah. Is there anything you can do for her?" Mila shouted, beating back the incoming fists with her shield.

"You mean like heal her?" Danica shouted in disbelief. "No way. Whoever she was, she died when something did this to her. There's not even an aura in there anymore."

Mila bit her lip, not liking what she knew she needed to do. She pressed the barrel of the Ivar to the heaving chest under her knee, making sure the heart was in the blast zone.

"I'm sorry about this," she whispered before pulling the trigger.

The sides of the pistol glowed with golden light for the briefest of moments before raw celestial magic was expelled from the barrel. There was a deep *thwump,* and the ground rumbled as a bolt of magic slammed into it after passing through the woman's chest.

With a shuddering scream, the elf's body shook and spasmed before seizing up. Mila was horrified to see the woman's nose and mouth begin to extend from her face in the shape of a muzzle and sprout thin black fur.

Mila was about to put another shot into her when the light faded from her eyes and she slumped to the ground, dead.

Mila slowly stood up and stared down at the thing. "What the fuck was that?"

"Shir shee chi!" Penny said, scaring the crap out of Mila as the dragon landed on her shoulder.

"Fucking hell!" Mila shouted, jumping backward and making Penny have to dig in her talons or fall off her shoulder. "Why the fuck would you scare me like that?" She pressed a fist to her chest and made a pained face. "Wait, did you just say she was a werewolf?"

CHAPTER EIGHT

"I'm not saying it *wasn't* a werewolf," Danica whispered as they crouch-walked through the thick underbrush. She was leading the way, her wood elf blood instinctively letting her know where to put her feet to keep quiet. Mila followed close behind, placing her feet in the same spots as Danica but managing to make twice as much noise as the elf.

"But in your medical opinion?" Mila said with a roll of her hand, prompting Danica to continue.

"Well, werewolves are intelligent," she said, moving a branch out of the way with the back of her hand. "That thing was nothing more than an animal. Plus, werewolves have a huge aura, and she didn't have anything. Almost like it had been stripped from her."

"Shir, chi chi," Penny argued from Mila's shoulder.

"Good point." Mila nodded. "If something had gone wrong when she was bitten or whatever, maybe she got all messed up. Besides, if she wasn't a werewolf, then what was she?"

Danica shrugged. "I don't know. I'm just saying, I don't think that was a werewolf. I think she was turning into something much more basic, like an animal. We're here," she said, cutting off further argument.

Mila moved up beside Danica at the edge of the forest, hunkering down behind a thatch of saplings to hide from view.

After checking the rest of the houses at the settlement and finding nothing more, they decided to check out the old logging camp Harvey had told them about. Mila was pretty sure the missing elves and Heather's disappearance were connected since the odds against it were astronomical. Mila was having trouble figuring out how not-were-wolves, a missing group of elves, and a potentially dead Valkyrie were connected, though. The only thing she knew for sure was that the woman who now owned the logging camp they were spying on was the last person to talk to Heather. If she could just figure out one of the threads, she knew the mystery sweater would unravel.

Mila had tried to call Preston to let him know that the settlement was destroyed, but she couldn't get any service on her phone, and the magical one Victoria had given her, while at full signal strength, only worked to contact the sisterhood. She figured if they were already out near the logging camp, they might as well get all the info they could before checking in with Preston.

So far, the only leads they had about the elves were that there might be a werewolf thing happening and several sets of drag marks led into the woods.

Unfortunately, Penny had only been able to follow the trail about a mile into the wood before the last set of drag marks disappeared, but they were heading in the general direction of the logging camp they were now staking out.

Ten minutes went by with nothing happening before Mila finally sat on the ground, giving up on the idea that she would need to move quickly anytime soon.

"Well, her car is parked over there, so at least we know she's here," Mila said, jutting her chin at the industrial sawmill leftover from the 40s that dominated the clearing. There were a few smaller buildings that looked like they had served a purpose at some time in the past, but they had mostly fallen into disrepair to the point of uselessness. A new Jeep Wrangler was parked in the grass beside the front entrance to the sawmill.

"Well, I guess it's better than fighting fucked up science experiments," Danica said, folding her legs under her and sitting in a pile of leaves without making a sound. "I'll take a little rest before we go running headfirst into who knows what next."

"I do not go running headfirst into things," Mila said, gently cuffing Danica's shoulder with the back of her hand.

"You're right. That's mostly your big dwarf man," Danica said, eliciting a hiccuping laugh from Penny that surprised the dragon as much as the two women.

"Chi chi?" Penny asked.

"Oh, he's probably chatting up pretty girls, asking if they've seen any gold bars lying around." Mila rolled her eyes.

"Jealous much?" Danica laughed.

"Yes," Mila snapped in mock anger. "Mostly of the fact that he's down in Mexico City having the time of his life while we're sitting here in the dirt waiting for a potential murderer to get bored and leave her sawmill."

———

Finn stood on the sidewalk of Avenida Hidalgo, adjusting the straps of the heavy-duty backpack he had just bought as he took in Alameda Central park. The park was the oldest in the city and happened to be less than a hundred feet from where a bar of Montezuma's gold had been found in the 80s.

Several pavilions were scattered throughout the well-manicured grounds, and people milled about on walks or played games with their children in the cool of late morning before the heat of the day really set in. In the center of the park was a large fountain that splashed water around a female statue in regal clothing and had a few children running through the cool waters.

Finn smiled as he took it all in. He liked to see people happy. Plus, things were about to get pretty gross for him.

Deciding he had wasted enough time, Finn clapped his hands together and slowly turned in a circle, looking for the closest manhole cover. Unfortunately, the closest was in the middle of Avenida Hidalgo, a fairly busy street. He considered finding an entrance to the sewers that was on a less busy street, but after considering his last couple of hours wandering through the huge city, he decided there wasn't anything like a *not* busy street in central Mexico City.

He waited for the streetlight to turn red and traffic to stop before he walked directly to the huge steel manhole cover that happened to be beside a large SUV with a family inside. A little girl in the back seat stared at him as he approached and gave him a tentative wave.

Finn smiled a huge toothy grin, waving at the little girl before pulling his beard like it was a doorbell rope. He popped his tongue out and crossed his eyes.

The little girl began to laugh, then stuck her thumbs in her ears and waggled her fingers at him. He retorted by pulling his nose up like a pig and sniffing around with wide eyes. The girl exploded with laughter and, putting her fingers under her eyes, pulled her cheeks down and rolled her eyes up into her head.

Finn laughed and took the opportunity to slip a finger of his prosthetic arm into one of the holes of the manhole cover. Flexing his back muscles, he easily lifted and slid the cover to the side. He was standing up again just as the little girl let go of her face and unrolled her eyes, giggling.

She looked at him expectantly but was confused when he pointed down at the road beside the car. Then he waved goodbye to her and stepped into the hole, dropping out of sight. Catching the ladder attached to the wall before falling too far, he reached up and slid the cover back into place before letting go of the ladder and dropping the twelve or so feet to the bottom.

He hit the ground in a solid-footed stance, but not before his feet passed through a literal river of shit that came up to his calves.

Finn gagged and almost threw up the breakfast tacos he had gotten from a street vendor thirty minutes ago before he got his guts under control. He took a couple of steadying breaths.

The unfortunate truth he was far too familiar with was that you could and would get used to any smell given enough time. He dreaded how bad he was going to stink when he got home.

After a few minutes, his dark vision was in full swing, and he could at least ignore most of the smells around him. He glanced both ways down the concrete tunnel that had a good eight-foot diameter and saw that there was a T junction about twenty feet behind him. The other way seemed to go on for quite a while, with only small inlets dotting the walls. As he watched a blast of water and other things shot out of one of the inlets.

"I'll go this way, I think," he said to himself, hiking a thumb over his shoulder in the opposite direction of the discharge.

Finn didn't know how his ability to find treasures worked. No dwarves did, but they knew it *did* work. No one could find a treasure like a dwarf who was actively looking for it. So, while choosing a direction to go in the sewer had more to do with not wanting to be sprayed with shit-water than it did with some mystical sense, he had to admit that the choice *felt* right.

Reaching the T junction, Finn looked left, then right. He didn't see a difference, so he went left.

"Man, I really wish I was sitting on the couch with Mila watching a movie," the dwarf grumbled as he sidestepped a particularly dense patch of human waste. "Must be nice just sitting around without a care in the world."

"Yeah, treasure hunting sounds like way more fun than this," Danica agreed.

"Chi," Penny said, pointing into the clearing.

Mila squinted and saw a red-haired woman in jeans and a long black duster coming out of the sawmill.

"We'll need to hurry back to the bike," Mila started but stopped when she saw the woman turn away from the Jeep and head toward the woods. "Or not. Where the hell is she going?"

"One way to find out," Danica suggested.

Mila chuckled. "I suppose there is."

"Shir chi," Penny said, taking off.

"Good call. We'll follow as close as we can. If you see us get lost, let us know which way to go."

Penny gave her a thumbs-up before shooting off into the woods, circling around to where the woman was heading.

"Let's go," Mila said, pointing in the direction Penny had flown off. "You lead the way, Miss Wood Elf."

"Oh, I was going to." Danica gave her a severe look. "You make more sound walking through the woods than Finn trying to meditate."

Mila chuckled. "Nothing is that loud."

CHAPTER NINE

Mila thought they had lost the trail, but Danica spotted the black-cloaked figure heading in a new direction just as Penny swooped down from the treetops and pointed her out before taking off once again.

Following in Danica's preternaturally quiet steps, Mila focused on her foot placement and left the following to Danica and Penny. She was surprised when Danica put a hand out to stop her. She looked up to see that they were at the edge of a ravine.

Danica pointed down into the ravine, which was a little over twenty feet wide at the base but ran off in either direction for several hundred feet like a gash in the forest floor. Mila looked over the edge and saw the woman walking down a path that had been carved into the granite walls. She was twenty feet from the bottom and just reaching the halfway mark on the path, putting the floor of the ravine at a good forty or more feet deep.

A quick scan of the opposite edge of the ravine and Mila spotted Penny hunkered down in some underbrush.

They made eye contact and Penny pointed straight down, drawing Mila's attention to the wall below the dragon's hiding place.

It took a second for her to realize she was looking at a cave, not just an overhang of rock blocking what little sunlight that made its way through the tree canopy. This was confirmed when the woman walked across the ravine bottom and through the opening, quickly swallowed by darkness.

"Okay, this officially just got creepy," Danica said quietly.

"Because she went into a cave?" Mila raised an eyebrow.

Danica nodded. "Name one good thing that's happened in a cave?"

"Yeah, good call." Mila bit her lip in consideration. "We need to see what's going on in there. Heather might still be alive and just being held captive. I don't like how the Sisterhood is just giving her up for dead."

"I understand that, but don't you guys, like, just get reborn?" Danica asked as Penny flew across the ravine and landed on Mila's shoulder.

"Not you too." Mila threw her hands up. "Yes, we get reborn, but the person we were is dead. If I die, yeah, I'll come back in twenty years or so, but I won't be Mila. I'll be some rando you've never met. We don't wake up until we're in our teens. Do you have any idea how much the first fifteen years of your life determines your personality? Victoria said Valkyries don't settle into a consistent personality until they hit their ninth or tenth life."

"Oh, I hadn't thought of that," Danica said with a frown.

"So, what you're saying is that in your next life, you might have some style sense?"

Mila snorted a laugh, slapping Danica's shoulder. "Don't be an asshole. That's Penny's job."

Penny's jaw dropped. "Chi?"

"Oh, don't give me that. We all know you're the asshole of the group." Mila pursed her lips, daring Penny to deny it.

A smoke ring from her nostril was all the answer Mila was going to get.

"Shir shee squee," Penny said, getting back down to business.

"Okay." Mila nodded, and Penny jumped off her shoulder and glided to the ravine floor. "She's going to see if the coast is clear for us to come down. Can you get a teleport spell ready in case we need to get out of here quickly?"

Danica nodded.

They watched Penny dart into the cave on foot, moving as quickly as a cat. After a few seconds, she came back out and waved her arms over her head.

"That's it. Let's go."

Mila, not worried about being heard, quickly ran to where the path cut into the wall started and carefully made her way down. She glanced back when she reached the halfway point and nearly jumped out of her skin when she saw Danica less than a foot behind her.

"Holy shit, you're so fucking quiet. You make ten times this much noise in the condo."

"I'm a wood elf. This is my natural environment."

Mila looked Danica up and down, noting the designer

black turtleneck and dark-orange leggings. She even had a gold necklace on, and knee-high boots.

"Yeah. Totally fit in here." Mila laughed. "You look like you just got out of yoga class."

"I'll have you know that orange and black blend with a forest surprisingly well. Hurry up, we're totally exposed on this wall." She shooed Mila on.

They reached the entrance of the cave, and Penny hopped onto Mila's shoulder. "Chi chi. Shir."

"She said the tunnel makes a few turns as it goes deeper. We need to be quiet. She heard talking and movement farther in," Mila translated, pulling out her Ivar and taking the lead.

The smell of wet dog and too many bodies mixed with the tangy smell of fresh-cut rock assailed Mila's senses as soon as she entered the large tunnel. The dark stone didn't reflect much of the light from outside, but Mila had noticed her vision in the dark was getting better—something that happened to Valkyries as they matured, according to Victoria. Mila still needed to hold a hand out in front of her to be sure she didn't walk into a wall, but she could see the basic shape of the tunnel as it quickly turned to the right.

She moved carefully, being sure not to kick any of the loose rocks that littered the floor down the passage. Danica's hand was on her back as she followed close behind, with Penny riding her shoulder.

The farther they went, Mila began to hear an almost girlish female voice speaking at a slightly raised volume as if speaking to a crowd. Light spilled around the next bend in the cave, and the smell of wet dog grew stronger.

The farther down the tunnel they went, the more magical heaviness there was in the air. Mila had felt that heaviness before when fighting the Dark Star; it was dark magic or something close to it.

"Do you feel that?" Mila asked quietly. "Is that magic?"

"Yeah, I feel it," Danica said with a shiver. "It feels like dark magic to me, but for it to be this thick?" She shivered again, shaking her head for emphasis.

"Squee shir. Chi chi, shir," Penny said.

"Infernal magic? Are you sure?" Mila asked, not liking the sound of "infernal."

"Are you kidding?" Danica whisper-shouted. "That's not possible. There are no infernal beings on Earth."

"Are you positive?" Mila asked.

Penny nodded.

"Shit."

Moving to the wall for cover, Mila inched her way up to the bend in the tunnel and peeked around it.

Her eyes widened and she gasped quietly.

"What is it?" Danica whispered, leaning forward.

Mila made room for her, and the elf took in the scene in the large chamber.

There were lights strung across the rough-cut ceiling, illuminating a crowd of half-man, half-wolf creatures standing in a tight pack at the center of the cavern. Mila counted at least thirty of the eight-foot-tall furry creatures, their wolf-like faces calm but still frightening in their monstrosity. They were facing away from where Mila and Danica watched, their attention on the woman in the long black coat.

The woman was standing on something so she was

77

above the gathered wolfmen and giving them a heartfelt speech.

"The Lord is waking and requires more sacrifice. We have a treat for him, but he must become more powerful to take it in. You are his children, like me before you, but the Lord has chosen me to be his hands and mouth in this new world. He came to me again in my dreams last night. It is time for speed. This Valkyrie was only the first of many to come to stop us." She pointed to the side, and Mila followed her finger to a figure secured to the wall with thick black chains.

Mila's hand went to her mouth. "Oh, my God. That's Heather."

"She's in a pretty bad state. These animals haven't been kind," Danica said harshly.

"Chi." Penny pointed to the back of the pack.

Mila saw what had caught Penny's attention. The wolfman closest to them was sniffing the air as if it was looking for something. The one beside it began to do the same thing. They bared their teeth and began to growl. The cave was suddenly filled with growls as the rest of the pack picked up on their fellows' warning.

The woman stopped speaking, sensing the shift in her wolfmen's attention.

"What do you smell, my darlings?" she asked in that creepy girlish voice.

The two wolfmen at the back of the crowd suddenly turned toward Mila and Danica, but Danica was quick and pulled Mila back out of sight.

"We need to get out of here," Danica said, holding her hands out and beginning to focus her magic.

"Heather is in there. We need to get her out," Mila argued.

"Shir shee," Penny said with a tight-lipped stare.

Mila nodded. "You're right. There are too many of them. Maybe I can get some help from Victoria."

The sound of scrambling feet told them that the wolfmen were heading their way. "Get us out of here, Danica."

A bubble formed around them as Mila saw a hairy snout come around the corner, but they were gone an instant later.

The next breath, they were crouching on the floor of their condo.

"Fuck. I think it saw us."

CHAPTER TEN

"What the hell was that?" Mila shouted, fishing her sisterhood-issued phone out of her pocket. "How on earth were so many werewolves in one place, and no one noticed?"

"Those weren't werewolves," Danica said, breathing fast. "They were only half-transformed. That's really painful for a werewolf, and they only do it if it gives them an advantage in battle. I think those were Rougarou."

Mila lowered the phone and raised an eyebrow at Danica. "What's a Rougarou?"

She blew a stray blonde hair out of her face as she headed for the fridge. "It's a thing that's halfway between a man and a wolf."

"No shit." Mila rolled her eyes and climbed onto one of the stools at the counter.

Danica pulled a couple bottled waters from the fridge and tossed one to Mila. Penny jumped off the elf's shoulder into the fridge to get herself a snack, so Danica left the door open and bent at the waist to lean her elbows on the counter. She cracked open the water and took a sip before continuing.

"They're not men who turn into a wolf or a wolf that turns into a man. They're an animal that is half-wolf and half-man or elf or whatever the victim used to be before it was changed."

"So, they're animals that used to be people?" Mila asked, horrified.

Danica nodded. "Yeah, and they're just about as smart as a wolf, which is pretty smart by the way, but they also have a geas placed upon them that compels them to follow their master's wishes to the best of their abilities. It's a terrible spell that will kill anyone who defies it. Honestly, it's the hardest part of creating a Rougarou. Changing someone's physical form isn't particularly hard unless something goes wrong and the person gets stuck, but only an idiot would let that happen."

"Can we save those people who have been turned into wolfmen?"

"Shir shee," Penny said, flying out of the fridge with a stack of deli meat and cheese in her arms. She kicked the door to close it and flew over to the island, landing between the two women.

Danica tore off a paper towel and put it at Penny's feet. Penny smiled at her and dropped the meat and cheese on the towel before stuffing a slice of turkey into her mouth.

"Why can't we change them back?" Mila frowned. "They were changed into animals, so they should be able to be turned back."

"Because their souls have been taken," Danica said with an apologetic shrug. "We could change them back, but they would already be dead. Well, to be honest, they wouldn't be dead, they would be more like zombies. The person for all intents and purposes is dead, even if the body is still alive."

Mila bit her lip while considering what to do. "We need to put them down, then. If we take out this woman and the Rougarou are free, they'll scatter and start attacking people at random. I'm giving Victoria a call. We need to get back there and save Heather before it's too late. Give me a minute."

Sliding off the stool, Mila paced across the room while she pulled up Victoria's contact info and hit send.

The phone picked up after two rings. "Mila, good to hear from you so soon. I take it the mission was quick?"

"Actually, we're in the middle of it still." Mila took a breath before plowing forward. "Look, I know you don't think it's that big of a deal, but Heather is still alive and being held captive. I know where she is, but I couldn't get her out. There's some crazy lady who has like thirty Rougarou under her control hiding out in some cave in the woods. Not to mention my friend Penny was sure she could feel infernal magic all throughout the place. I think something really big is going down."

Victoria was quiet on the other line for long enough that Mila checked to be sure the call was still connected. "Are you there?"

"Yes, dear." She took a deep breath before continuing. "I know you are new to this life, but in that time, you have seen more than most. However, what you are saying has some issues to it."

"How so?" Mila asked cautiously.

"First, there is no way your friend felt infernal magic.

83

There is no being on Earth that can produce Infernal magic. The last one was dealt with by the sisterhood; I landed the final blow myself. We are always on the lookout for infernals, but we haven't found anything in thousands of years.

"Second, while Rougarou are a thing, and they do come about from time to time, there is no way there are thirty of them under one woman's control. At most, a practitioner of dark magic could have five Rougarou under their control. What you saw were more than likely werewolves in their middle state.

"I'm sorry, dear, but what you're proposing is ludicrous."

Mila bit her cheek to keep from telling Victoria off. She knew what she had seen. "What about Heather? I know where she is. We can go and save her."

Victoria sighed. "I understand why you want to save her, but your opinions will change after you've lived a few lifetimes. She's dead, dear. We can't take the chance of exposing ourselves by getting too involved. Our first mandate is to keep the Reaper safe."

"This is fucking bullshit," Mila exploded. "How dare you patronize me? I don't give a shit if Heather will be born again, she's still alive right now. You keep telling me how important the sisterhood is, but when one of our own is in trouble, we just abandon them? Why? Because you don't want to expose a weapon you created? We keep the fucking Reaper in the Elsewhere! How can it be stolen when it's not even here on Earth? You need to suck it up and do something. Now, what you're going to do is meet me in the fucking woods in northern Idaho and see that what I'm saying is the truth."

Victoria chuckled darkly. "Fine. I'll meet you there."

Mila blinked a few times in surprise. "Really?"

"Yes, really."

"Do you need to know where the cave is?"

"No, I can see where it is from your phone's location. I'll meet you there in half an hour," Victoria said, a smile in her voice.

"Okay. Half an hour. See you then." Mila hit the end call button.

"That was fucking intense," Danica said, making Mila turn. She and Penny were eating deli meat and watching Mila like she was the best thing on TV.

"Yeah, I guess it was." Mila laughed. "I need to call Preston next."

"You want me to make us some lunch?"

"Chi."

"Yeah, we know you want lunch, Penny." Danica laughed as she went to the fridge.

Mila put the sisterhood's phone in one pocket and pulled her normal one out of the other. After finding Preston's number, she hit send and prepared herself for another intense conversation.

"Mila. I didn't think I would hear back so soon." Preston's baritone rumbled out of the phone, tickling her ear.

"So, we found the settlement."

"From your tone, it wasn't good."

Mila swallowed and told him what they had found. She

skipped the detail about Heather and her part in it all, but she told him about the Rougarou and the woman.

"I'll send a G.A.E.L. team up to take care of it. I should have a team available in a few days," Preston said with a sigh. "It's a shame about the settlement. They were good people."

"Actually, is there a way to free up one of the teams sooner?" Mila asked, crinkling her nose.

"I suppose I could. Why?"

"There's someone being held captive, and I'm pretty sure the Rougarou are going to start hunting more people soon. I'm heading up there now and can get more info."

"I don't know that I like you going back there without backup." Preston's voice was full of fatherly concern.

"Don't worry, I have plenty of backup for a scouting mission. I'll be careful."

She heard him take in a deep breath and blow it out slowly. "Okay, I'll get on pulling a team back here as soon as possible. Call me and let me know where you are as soon as you've done your scouting."

"Okay, I will. Thanks, Preston."

"No problem." He sighed. "Mila, be careful."

She chuckled. "Now you sound like Finn."

"Why do you think I want you to be careful?"

"Because of Finn?" she asked, raising an eyebrow. "What does he have to do with it?"

"You're out on a mission for me. If something happens to you, who do you think he's going to blame?"

She laughed. "I think you'll be fine. You're a fucking Minotaur."

"I may be a Minotaur, but he's a fucking dwarf king

berserker. He would tear my house down to get to me, and it's not even finished yet." He chuckled. "Just be careful so we don't have to see what he would do to me in retaliation."

"I promise. I'll be careful," Mila said, crossing her fingers.

CHAPTER ELEVEN

Mila sat at the kitchen island, cracking open her water bottle and taking a long drink.

"Preston's on board?" Danica asked, dumping a box of mac and cheese noodles into a pot of boiling water on the stove.

"Yeah, he'll have a team ready for us at some point." Mila laughed. "First time for everything, I guess."

"Went better than your chat with Victoria."

"Shee," Penny agreed with an eye roll.

Mila felt her dark mood come back in a flash. "I just don't get how she can so callously let her sisters die. We know Heather's alive! We saw her."

"I mean, she's really old." Danica shrugged. "When you live that long, you get weird. Even elves get weird after a few hundred years, and we're used to it."

"Yeah, I get it, but it doesn't make it right."

"Okay, I understand that you don't want to let her die, but," she held up her hands to forestall an argument, "why are you so sure she's wrong? I mean, Victoria has known

Heather for thousands of years. How do you know Victoria doesn't know what Heather would want?"

Mila pressed her lips together as she took the time to think that over. "It's because I learned about fighting evil from Finn. Not in the way that he charges in headfirst, but in the way that he can't abide it. The issue is simple. There is someone who needs to be saved, and we know about it. That means we're obligated to do something."

Danica nodded, stirring the boiling noodles. "Yeah, he is all about doing the right thing. He's just so put together when facing a problem."

"It's that quiet confidence," Mila agreed.

Penny rolled her eyes and chuckled.

The wall crumbled under the insistent boot of Finn. Concrete and stone exploded inward as his foot came through the wall.

Raw sewage poured out of the hole as Finn stumbled forward, coughing and falling to his knees. His stomach contracted and he fought to keep his breakfast down, but as it passed his uvula, he knew there was no stopping it. He spewed tacos across the roughly paved floor of the chamber.

He spat the last remains of tortilla out of his mouth and swallowed hard. Taking a few deep breaths, his hands on his knees, Finn focused on the relatively fresh air. After getting to the point that he was fairly certain he wasn't going to vomit again, he scanned the room.

His brows rose when he saw how big the chamber was.

Rows of eight-foot-thick columns held up the ceiling that soared into the darkness. The room was so large he couldn't see the other side. Glancing left and right, he couldn't see the sides either.

"How fucking big is this place?" Finn grumbled as he climbed to his feet.

The stink of sewage made him wrinkle his nose and move deeper into the chamber. After a dozen steps, a sound made him stop and cock his head to listen.

It took him a few seconds to understand what he was hearing, but when he did, he immediately pulled Fragar from its holster and whispered the power word. The axe unfolded in the blink of an eye as fifty two-foot-tall ratmen came out of the dark.

They ran on their hind legs and wore scraps of leather as armor. Each had some sort of weapon in their hands, from short swords to a simple club, and all of them began chattering war cries in their language.

"Holy shit!" Finn shouted in surprise. Then he smiled.

Hefting his axe, he began sprinting toward the incoming pack. "LET'S DO THIS, RAT-FUCKERS!"

With a pop, Mila, Danica, and Penny appeared in the middle of the woods beside a fallen tree with several smaller trees growing from the dead trunk.

Mila glanced around, trying to get her bearings. "Where are we?"

"I didn't want to teleport us directly to the cave in case they were waiting for us," Danica said, pointing. "The ravine is over that way a couple hundred meters. This was the closest landmark I could remember."

"I wonder if Victoria is here?" Mila said, starting toward the cave.

"I'm here," a deep, sultry voice said from above and behind them.

Mila spun, her Ivar out and pointing at a tall blonde woman with tan skin and a muscular build. She wore a pair of dark green form-fitting hiking pants and a red and black plaid flannel shirt. Her hair was up in an intricate braid that had been pinned to her head in a spiral pattern, giving the impression of a lot of hair being styled as compactly as possible. There was also the hilt of a long sword peeking over her right shoulder.

"Victoria?" Mila said, lowering the gun. She had only seen the woman twice back when she had been able to go to Elsewhere, before she'd used the Reaper to save the woman who had become the Dark Star. Since then, she had only spoken to Victoria on the phone, and even then, the conversations were brief due to the woman having very little time to herself since she ran some large corporation. Mila realized she still didn't know what Victoria's company did besides make shit-tons of money.

"Yes, dear. It's me." She smiled, hopping down from the fallen cedar tree and holding out a hand to Danica. "You must be Danica Meadows. I'm Victoria Gara." They shook hands with a single solid pump before Victoria glanced at Penny, sitting on Mila's shoulder. "And you must be Penny. Wonderful to meet you. There hasn't been a proper dragon on Earth for quite some time."

"Shir shee, squee," Penny said, putting her hands on her hips.

Victoria raised a manicured brow. "I'm sorry, I don't speak draconic."

Mila turned a little red but translated. "She said, 'Not that *you* know of.' She can be a little," Mila gave Penny a hard look, "opinionated. Sorry."

Victoria smiled. "It's not a problem. She's right, I'm assuming there aren't any dragons because I haven't seen or heard about any for the last thousand years. There very well could be one or two in hiding."

It wasn't so much an admission of wrongness as a statement that she knew better. Mila picked up on it, and so did Penny.

"Chi shir," Penny said, crossing her arms.

Victoria raised an eyebrow and looked to Mila for a translation.

Mila suddenly understood what Finn went through when he had to translate for the opinionated dragon. While Mila agreed with Penny that Victoria was being a bitchy know it all, she couldn't say that to her mentor.

"She said we should get moving," Mila said, giving Penny a pleading glance to keep her mouth shut. But to Mila's surprise, Penny didn't even flinch at the blatant mistranslation. Realization hit Mila in the face like a wet sock; Finn did this all the time, and Penny expected it. How many times had Penny made some scathing comment that Finn just played off?

Mila narrowed her eyes at Penny. "This is your real game, isn't it?" Mila whispered as they all set out, Danica in the lead.

Penny gave her an amused half-smile and winked.

They made their way to the edge of the ravine and hunkered down as Penny went to scout the area. She came out of the cave and gave the all-clear, a frown on her tiny face.

Taking the cut path to the ravine's bottom, Mila held out her hand for Penny to climb up her arm. "What is it?"

Penny explained, shrugging at the end.

"What is it?" Victoria asked.

"She says the caves are empty," Mila growled before marching into the opening, the others following close behind her.

"I'm not surprised," Victoria said, holding out her hand and creating a ball of light in her palm before tossing it into the air, where it floated and followed along beside her. "Werewolves are fairly nomadic when the pack is young and growing. Too many people going missing from the surrounding area draws too much attention. They probably saw Heather coming to investigate as a sign that they had overstayed their welcome."

"I'm telling you, those were not werewolves," Mila said, frustrated with the elder Valkyrie.

"I know what you think you saw, Mila, but once you have a few lives under your belt, you'll understand better how things work. You've only known about the magical world for less than a year. These things take time."

Mila ground her teeth but decided arguing about it wasn't going to do them any good. Instead, she led the way to the corner she and Danica had hidden at less than an hour ago and peeked around the corner.

The large chamber was empty and dark. She listened,

but there was no sound to give away anyone waiting to jump out and ambush them.

Victoria had no such concerns and walked around the corner and into the chamber, her orb casting harsh white light across bare walls and floors. Even the lights across the ceiling were gone. It was clean. Like, really clean. Too clean for a cave. But there was no trace of anyone having been there, especially not in the last hour.

"I don't get it," Mila said, walking into the chamber. She went to the wall where she had seen Heather chained up, but there wasn't even a hole where the chains had been secured. "She was right here."

"I don't feel the magical oppression that was here the first time," Danica said, slowly taking in the empty chamber. "It's like the whole place has been scrubbed clean."

"As I said, they probably moved on when they realized we were coming after them. Mila, you did a fine job tracking down the problem. The corruption we detected was probably from the werewolves. They all have a taint, and in large groups, they can give the impression of a dark magic-user. I am sad that our sister will have to go through another cycle so soon, but it is part of being a Valkyrie. I have spent all the time I can on this, unfortunately. I have obligations back home that I must attend too. We shall talk again on Friday. I'll let Missy know you did more than your due diligence."

She walked over to Mila and put a hand on her cheek in a motherly fashion. "I know you wanted to do more for her, but this is the way things go for us most of the time. It's a fact of the life of a Valkyrie. Now, I must leave. Being close to you is draining my power at a prodigious rate. I'm sorry, my dear, but there's nothing more to be done."

Mila wanted to say more, but she knew it would fall on deaf ears. She nodded and held out a hand, indicating that Victoria should lead the way. "After you."

They headed out of the cave and back into the early afternoon light. Mila squinted, holding up a hand to shade her eyes from the bright sun as she let her eyes adjust.

"It was a pleasure to meet you, Danica. You as well, Penny. Please take care of my sister while she is with you in this life." Victoria gave them both a short bow before turning to Mila. "Take the rest of the day off; you earned it. This was excellent work, dear. I'll talk to you on Friday."

She stepped back from the group and held out her arms, her eyes closed. Mila raised an eyebrow in confusion, then jumped back with a yelp as what looked like a lightning bolt shot from Victoria, consuming her completely. The bolt shot half a mile into the air, taking the tall blonde woman with it. They watched it travel up in the blink of an eye before it made a ninety-degree turn and headed east faster than they could track.

Mila stomped on the ground, sending a loose stick flipping through the air. "I fucking *hate* being patronized! Just because she's so fucking old, she thinks she knows everything. The only thing I think her old age has given her is a complacent attitude. Just because you haven't seen it before doesn't mean it isn't possible. Fuck!"

"So, are we done then?" Danica asked, letting Mila stomp out her fury without trying to stop her.

"Fuck, no!" Mila looked up at her friend, her fists

clenched in anger. "I know what I saw. We're seeing this through to the end."

"That's my girl." Danica smiled. "So, what's next?"

Mila's rage deflated. "I have no idea."

"Shee shir. Chi chi," Penny reminded them.

"Oh, yeah. I suppose we should return Harvey's motorcycle," Mila said with a shiver. "Can we at least drive at a reasonable speed on the way back to town?"

Danica laughed. "Normally I'd say no, but you've had a hard day. I'll give you a break."

Mila snorted. "That's more than I deserve, considering how many times you've had to tell me to slow down in the Hellcat."

CHAPTER TWELVE

Danica kept the bike under fifty and didn't complain when Mila cinched down on her torso to keep herself from falling off the back. They drove the five miles to town, mostly on paved roads that were in desperate need of repair. The dirt roads were smoother than the paved.

When they were about a mile from town, Penny gave the signal that she was going to fly ahead. Mila gave her a thumbs-up before quickly wrapping her arm back around Danica.

"You doing okay back there?" the elf shouted over her shoulder.

"I'm fine," Mila shouted in reply over the constant buzz of the motor.

There were still in the rather thick coverage of the woods. The road, which had been laid down in the early 30s, was barely wide enough for two cars to pass one another, and the forest had grown right up to the edge of the lane, making the ride a little more claustrophobic than normal.

Mila saw Penny come swooping in from above. She was moving fast and banked hard to come up behind them. With a burst of speed, she surged forward, grabbed the back of Mila's jean jacket, and crawled up so she could speak in her ear.

"Shir squee! Chi shir."

"Fucking hell. Danica, step on it," Mila shouted. "Penny says the town is under attack by the Rougarou."

Danica twisted her wrist and the bike lurched forward, making Mila hold on tight as they quickly passed seventy miles an hour. Mila could see the bright sliver of light where the tree line gave out coming up fast.

The bike buzzed like a thousand wasps in a jar, working as hard as it could to get them to town in time.

"How many are there?" Mila asked Penny, who still clung to her back.

"Chi."

"What did she say?" Danica asked, focused on the road ahead.

"All of them," Mila answered as they shot out of the relative darkness of the forest road and out into the clearing behind the bar that sat on the main drag.

The road was overgrown with grass, really more of the idea of a path than a road, and the bike went airborne as they hit patches of thick grass growing from the crumbling pavement.

Mila sucked in a breath when she saw the Rougarou terrorizing the town. It looked like there was one or two at each house or business, tearing chunks out of walls and kicking doors in. They frothed at the mouth and howled loud enough that she could hear them over the bike's motor.

"Park at the bar. I have an idea," Mila said, pointing to the red one-story building.

Danica nodded and leaned the bike toward the building, taking them off-road—not that Mila could tell the difference. Locking the back brake up, Danica swung the ass end of the dirt bike into a slide and put the kickstand down as they came to a stop in the gravel lot of the bar.

Mila pushed off the back and took off toward the dumpster as soon as her feet hit the ground. "Cover me for a second. I'm sure the sound of the bike will bring them running."

Penny launched herself from Mila's back to join Danica, while Mila ran for the corner of the building where she had seen the huge yellowjacket nest when they first got there.

"God, I hope this works," Mila said to herself as she slid to a stop in front of the dumpster and started waving her arms above her head. "Hello! Mr. Yellowjacket! Hello!"

There was a pulse in the back of Mila's mind as her nature affinity kicked in and she gained the attention of the yellowjackets guarding the nest's entrance. They turned their black eyes to her and cocked their heads, considering her.

"Look, I know you and humans in general have a bad relationship, but right now, I could really use your help," Mila said, glancing over her shoulder to see Danica loose an arrow. A yelp not unlike a dog's followed, letting Mila know Danica had hit her mark.

The yellowjackets put their heads together for a second, then one of them crawled into the nest's opening. Mila didn't know exactly what they were saying, but she got the general idea. A feeling of "patience" filled her head. She didn't know if she couldn't understand them completely because they were workers, or if they were not trying to communicate with her directly.

Over the last few months, the one ability that had grown by leaps and bounds was Mila's nature affinity. All Valkyries had one, but no two were alike. Mila's was an ability to communicate with insects. She had always had the ability to some degree, even when she was a little girl, but up until about six months ago, it had been nothing but feelings and gestures from the insects. When she had come into her power, however, she had started to understand them. It wasn't an exact understanding, and when she tried to explain it to Finn, the best she could do was to compare it to the way Penny spoke. Not exactly a language, but a mix of language and magic and body movements.

Mila pulled her Ivar out and switched the safety off before whispering her power word for her armor. After a second's consideration, she pulled out Gram as well and held the handle close to her mouth, whispering a second power word. The gold sword unfolded in a flash, glowing with magical light as it fully formed.

The sword had been a gift from Finn, along with her armor. The dwarven sword was close to three feet in length and looked to be made of solid gold, but it weighed only ounces and held an edge that could shave the hair from Mila's arm without a problem. It was also the sword that had slain the dragon Fafnir, who ironically was a dwarf who had been turned into a dragon by a magical ring, then killed by his own sword. He was also Finn's ancestor.

Buzzing made Mila look up in time to see several hundred yellowjackets come out of the nest's opening and hover in the air before the queen flew out and shook herself as if stretching. She turned to Mila and flew a few feet closer.

"My workers tell me you have something to ask of me," the queen hummed, or at least that was how Mila heard it.

"Yes. The town is being attacked by large wolf-like creatures. They're going to take all the people from here. Will you send out soldiers to attack them for me?" Mila asked, wanting to get moving but not looking away from the queen as she considered, even when she heard another yelp of pain from behind her.

"Why would I sacrifice my brood for your people?" the queen asked.

Mila simply pointed at the dumpster, where a pair of worker yellowjackets crawled out of it as if making her point for her. "Because if my people go away, so does the easy source of food. Your nest is large and powerful because of the waste these people leave for you. They go, and your nest will collapse. You'll run out of food."

The queen considered for only a moment, seeing that Mila was right. "Very well. I will send half my soldiers to help. What do you need from them?"

"Swarm the wolfmen that are carrying people and sting them until they drop the person. Inflict as much damage as possible. We need to drive them away."

The queen dipped, then flew back into her massive

hive. A few seconds later, thousands of yellowjackets swarmed out of the nest and flew around the corner in a long stream of black and yellow bodies. It was honestly horrifying.

Mila tuned and ran to Danica, Penny on her shoulder. She saw there was one dead Rougarou on the ground in the gravel drive between the bar and the building beside it. "You okay?"

Danica nodded. "Killed this one with a shot to the throat, and put an arrow in another's leg. They go down easy enough, although they look strong as hell."

They jogged toward the main street, Mila taking the lead. "Cover me. Penny, watch our backs. Those things are fast," she said as a Rougarou shot out from between a yellow 1940s house and its cinderblock detached garage.

The wolfman took one look at them and bared its teeth before sprinting toward them. Mila didn't think twice. She aimed the pistol and pulled the trigger. A sucking of magic in the back of her head made her narrow her eyes in pain, but a bolt of gold light lanced out of the barrel and punched a hole through the charging beast's chest. It died between strides, tipping forward and sliding to a stop at Mila's feet.

"Try to stop the ones with people in their arms, but for fuck's sake, don't hit the captives," Mila shouted, taking aim at another Rougarou, this one loping across the street with an elf woman slung over its shoulders.

Another blast of raw magic and the Rougarou's legs were gone at the waist. The torso fell to the ground, sending the elf woman rolling away as she continued to scream. Only when the beast didn't come after her did she realize it had been killed.

"Get to the bar. We'll send anyone we find that way," Danica shouted to the woman as she let an arrow fly. The missile struck a Rougarou in the small of its back, severing its spine. The man in its grasp tumbled away.

The woman nodded and ran to the newly freed man, pulling him up and helping him to the bar behind Mila and Danica.

Mila watched as a black cloud of yellowjackets descended on a wolfman as it tried to make a run for the forest, its prey in hand. Within seconds the beast had dropped the man, who scrambled away as it was repeatedly stung by thousands of wasps, their yellow bodies standing out against the black fur. When the hulking figure finally stopped moving, the yellowjackets lifted off the dead wolfman as one and flew to their next victim.

Mila sprinted to a house where a Rougarou was struggling with the occupant, but before she could get there, a bubble formed around the wolfman's head. It staggered back to fall off the porch and into the small front yard. It kicked and ripped at the bubble, but to no avail.

A man came out of the house, a wand in his right hand aimed at the Rougarou's head. "How do you like that, you fucking pup?" he asked in a proper English accent. He saw Mila and Danica and waved them away. "No worries, ladies. I have this one in the drink."

Mila saw that the bubble was actually a sphere of water, and the Rougarou was well on its way to drowning. "I see that you do. Uh, you should head for the bar when you're done here. That's where we're sending survivors. They could use a fighter like you."

He chuckled darkly. "I was already headed there. Nice to know I'll have company. Ladies." He tipped an imaginary hat and started toward the bar, a wobble in his step and the smell of gin wafting off him. The bubble popped and water splashed around the Rougarou's head, but the beast didn't move, already dead.

"This is a really weird fuckin' town, Mila," Danica said, shaking her head.

A long high-pitched whistle sounded, cutting through the screams and growls of the beasts. As if a switch had been flipped, the Rougarou turned and sprinted for the woods. A good third of them still had victims in their arms. Danica was able to hit two of the retreating wolfmen in the thighs. One dropped the screaming woman it held, but the other was able to keep hold and vanished into the trees at a limping gallop.

Within seconds it was over, the only sign of the retreating Rougarou a high keening wail that was picked up by the remaining pack as they made their escape.

"So, we're *not* going home?" Danica asked.

"Not just yet," Mila confirmed as Penny landed on her shoulder. "Can you follow them?"

Penny nodded. "Chi."

"Can you follow them safely?" Mila amended.

"Chi shir?"

Mila rolled her eyes. "Safe for *you*."

Penny nodded. "Chi."

"Okay, we'll be at the bar with everyone else." Mila held out her fist. "Be careful."

Penny bumped the offered fist and took off.

"She's just so cocky," Danica said, watching the little dragon as she grew smaller.

"Good thing she's not a male."

"Why's that?" Danica asked, frowning.

"Because her balls would weigh her down too much to fly."

CHAPTER THIRTEEN

"Mila! Danica!"

They turned to find Harvey jogging up, his hand to his head and blood running down his cheek and neck, but otherwise looking unhurt. Danica immediately slung her bow over her shoulders and formed a bubble around herself.

"Be right back," she said before the bubble popped and she was gone.

"Uh, okay," Mila said to the empty air where her friend had just been.

Harvey came to a stop and pressed a hand to his scalp, putting pressure on a pretty bad cut if the amount of blood was an indication. His previously white t-shirt was now half-red, and the top of his well-fitting jeans had a dark bloodstain on one side.

"Where did Danica go? The blood scare her off?" he asked, wide-eyed.

"I have no idea, but I know it wasn't the blood since

she's a doctor. This kind of stuff is her bread and butter. Well, she mostly deals with kids, but still."

"What the hell happened? I was getting the bar set up for tonight, and all of a sudden, the front door was kicked in by a fuckin' werewolf. We haven't had werewolves around here since the 80s. Why were they stealing people? And why the hell didn't they change completely? That had to hurt, to walk around half-formed like that." He was rambling, but Mila gave him a pass since he was more than likely in a state of shock.

Blood loss like he'd had could cause all sorts of problems, including wooziness, which his swaying indicated.

"Harvey, I think we need to talk inside. You don't look so hot," Mila said, stepping to his side and trying to take some of his weight. She was so short, though, that she ended up hugging him around the waist. Hooking her fingers around his belt, she was able to keep him relatively steady as they headed for the red building a block and a half down the road.

A popping sound made Mila look over her shoulder. Danica had reappeared, and she had her medical bag over her shoulder. She spotted them and jogged to catch up, taking Harvey's weight on the other side. She was tall enough that his arm rested on her shoulders, making the task much easier for her.

"Sorry, had to grab my bag. I take it we're headed for the bar?"

"I should have guessed," Mila said, nodding. "Yeah, we're headed for the bar. How are you doing, Harvey?"

"Okay, I suppose. Now that the adrenaline is wearing off, I'm getting a little weak."

Danica stopped them and had Harvey sit in the road. "I need to take care of this now. No sense letting him pass out."

She pulled a spray bottle off saline out and ripped open a fresh package of gauze. Gently moving Harvey's hand away from the wound, she began spraying it down with saline to see what she was working with.

"Mila," Harvey said, reaching for her hand, "they took a bunch of my people. We're not fighters up here. Most of us came here because we wanted a simple life. We don't have a Market or any other connection to the rest of the magical community. I know you have a relationship with Meri-wether. Is there any way you can convince him to send some help so I can get my people back? Those monsters are going to eat them alive or something, I just know it."

"Calm down, Harvey," Mila reassured him. "Preston is already working on getting me some people. I'll need to use a phone to call him, though. My cell doesn't work up here."

"I have a phone in the bar—" He sucked in a breath of pain as Danica pressed the two halves of his scalp together.

She closed her eyes, and her hands began to glow with a blue light Mila had become familiar with. She was channeling her elven healing magic into the wound. Her artificial hand glowed a magnitude brighter, all the magic channeled through it visible in its woven diamond lattice. After a few seconds, the glow diminished, and she removed her hands, spraying the area down one last time to get rid of any residual blood so she could check her work.

"The wound is healed, but you still lost a lot of blood. We need to get some food in you, and you need to take it easy for a day or two while you recover." Danica stood and helped Harvey to his feet, steadying him with an arm around the waist. "Come on, let's get you inside."

They made their way to the bar without much problem, though Harvey did almost trip twice, and Mila had to help keep him steady.

Pushing the heavy wooden door open, Mila wasn't surprised at the interior in the least. It was the classic small-town bar: lots of wood, and a dingy red carpet that had last been cleaned in the 70s. There were two pool tables in the back section and a long dark-wood bar along the right side, opposite a set of bathrooms. The middle area was cleared for a relatively new wooden dance floor, and round tables with simple wooden chairs filled in all the rest of the available space. It looked like they could fit the entire population of the town in the place at once, and Mila guessed they did so on the regular.

There were already a dozen people inside, most injured in some way and being taken care of by their friends and family. Several people were openly crying and not always from their injuries.

Danica and Mila helped Harvey to a stool at the bar, where he nearly collapsed onto the wooden bar top. He pointed a shaky finger at an old cream-colored phone that looked like it had come out of a 1980s TV show prop room.

"There's the phone. Can you grab me a beer or something? I'm really thirsty," he said drunkenly.

"Give him water and find something for him to eat. I'm going to help the rest of these people." Danica patted him on the back. "Don't worry, Harvey, we'll have you drinking beer again in no time. For now, just do what Mila tells you."

She glanced around the room, quickly assessing who needed the most help first, then heading off to a table with a young elf with a severely broken arm, digging out what she needed from her bag as she went.

Mila opened one of the coolers behind the bar and didn't see any bottled water, so she went to the next. In the third cooler, she found a small stack of waters and grabbed a couple. On the wall was a rack with snacks, and she snatched a couple of packages of cookies before heading back to Harvey.

"Here, eat these," she said, dropping the cookies and waters off in front of him before lifting the heavy telephone onto the bar and pulling her phone out of her pocket.

As Harvey slowly tore open the first pack of cookies, she scrolled through her phone until she found Preston's contact info. Lifting the receiver, she punched in the number and turned her phone's screen off when the line started ringing.

"Mila?" Preston asked, his voice concerned.

She blinked. "How did you know it was me? I'm calling from a landline."

"The caller ID said the Red Brick Tavern, which is the name of the only bar in Elk River. I assumed if anyone was calling me from Elk River, it would be you."

"Well, aren't you the clever one?"

He chuckled. "I'm not a billionaire by chance, Mila."

"Fair enough," she conceded. "Listen, it's gotten really bad up here. The Rougarou I told you about? They just attacked the town. Broke into the homes and started stealing people. About half of the town was taken if I had to guess. I need that G.A.E.L. team asap."

"They attacked in broad daylight?" He sounded incensed. "I'm glad I went with my gut on this one. I recalled a team right away. One of the missions I had wasn't as time-sensitive as we first thought, and I brought them back. They're eating a quick meal now, but I'll inform them that they need to get moving now. You said they took the townsfolk alive? Why?"

"I've been thinking about that," Mila said, opening one of the waters and taking a drink to wet her dry mouth. She looked at Harvey and turned away, talking in a low voice so he wouldn't hear. "When Penny, Danica, and I first found them, I heard their leader talking about her 'Lord.' At first, I thought she was just some religious nut or something, but now I think she might be using people as an actual sacrifice. Obviously, the Rougarou are the bodies of her victims, but I don't understand what she's trying to accomplish."

Preston was silent as he thought. "Do you know where they are keeping the townsfolk?"

"Not yet, but Penny is following them now. Hopefully, she can tell us when she gets back."

"Okay, the team will be teleporting there in the next fifteen minutes. I'll let them know you're in charge. Clean these Rougarou out. They are not going to be stopped otherwise. And Mila?"

"I know," she said, rolling her eyes, "I'll be careful." She hung up the phone and turned to see Harvey working on the second pack of cookies.

She put her head in her hands and groaned. "God, I wish I was with Finn, having a grand old time treasure hunting. He's got all the luck today."

———

Dead ratmen littered the floor all around Finn as he took in long, even breaths, getting his rage under control. Looking over his shoulder, he could see a trail of the dead minions leading back into the darkness where he had started the long trek across the gigantic chamber.

He turned back to the opening in the wall in front of him. It was an open set of double doors made of foot-thick stone. Beyond them was a cube-shaped room thirty feet to a side. His dark vision could just make out a row of ten pillars against the far wall, each of them with a section that rotated and was marked with half a dozen pictographs. In the center of the pillars was another set of double doors, but these were shut tight.

Finn sighed. It was a puzzle. He hated puzzles. That was why he and Penny made such a good team. He did the killing, she did the thinking.

"Fuck it." He groaned. "How hard can it be?"

He looked down at his blood-soaked clothing and picked a chunk of ratman off his forearm, flicking it onto the ground.

"I hate minions," he muttered before striding into the cube-shaped puzzle room.

As soon as he got to the halfway point, the doors behind him slammed shut.

He spun, his guard up, but there was no enemy, and he relaxed—until a scraping sound made him look up.

Footlong spikes lowered from the ceiling.

"Oh, come on!"

Then the ceiling started descending slowly, intent on crushing him if he didn't solve the puzzle in time.

"Great. No pressure, Finn." He turned back to the pillars and tried to figure out how to solve the damn thing.

He went to the first pillar and started rotating it, looking at each picture. There was a man fishing, a dog jumping over a fence, what looked like a bird taking a crap on a man's head, two people either sword fighting with really short swords or two people touching penises—he couldn't tell which—and finally, a picture of a ratman pooping off a cliff.

He rotated through the pictures again.

He roared in frustration, "I fucking *hate* puzzles!"

CHAPTER FOURTEEN

Mila stacked another table against the window to the left of the Red Brick Tavern's front door. Harvey slid a chair up behind her and carefully went for another, wobbling only slightly, while Mila wedged the chair into the rickety barricade they had built.

"I don't think this is going to hold against a pack of Rougarou," Mila said, shaking the stack and having to steady it before is all tumbled to the floor. "They wouldn't even need to huff and puff. They could just call it a bad name, and it would come tumbling down."

Harvey chuckled at the bad joke but waved her back. "Let me finish it up before you judge too harshly."

Holding out a hand, he furrowed his brow and concentrated as his palm began to glow with golden light. The bar filled with the smell of rain, and a string of small bubbles began to pour out of the light from his hand and zip across the room to attach to the barricade. The bubbles came faster and faster, slowly filling the gaps. When bubbles filled all the spaces and bound the tables and chairs together, they began to pop, leaving light gray concrete behind. Within a minute or two, the barricade was made of tables, chairs, and a shit-ton of solid concrete.

Mila nodded. "You were right. The finishing touches really brought the whole thing together."

Harvey laughed, went to the makeshift barricade on the other side of the door, and repeated the process.

Mila looked over the preparations they had made. The back door was made of steel and had two crossbars holding it closed, which was about as secure as they could make it in the tight space. The two barricades covered the only two windows in the bar, but the front door was going to be a problem.

The door was just a simple wooden door with a window in the top half. Mila was pretty sure she could kick it in, given half a chance. A Rougarou would break it down with one swipe of its claws.

"What's your plan for the front door?" Mila asked, looking over her shoulder at Harvey.

He gave a defeated shrug. "We'll just have to use it as a choke point and fight them off. We can't seal it up until everyone is in here. If you can free the rest of the towns-people, they will make a beeline for here. This is the designated fallback point."

"What about when everyone is here?"

"I guess I'll concrete it up like the windows. We'll have to see what works best. I don't want to leave any of my people out there."

Mila nodded. "I can understand that." Mila looked around the bar at the two dozen people sitting in small groups. "How many know offensive magic?" she asked quietly.

He glanced around the room before turning back to her. "Not many. Like I said, most people moved out here to live a peaceful life. There are a few, though. We can do some damage if we need to."

Mila started to reply but was interrupted when two large bubbles appeared and instantly popped, leaving a small group of people in black tactical gear standing in the center of the bar's dance floor. A few of the townsfolk let out yelps or screams but calmed down quickly when Mila approached the heavily armed men and women with a large smile on her face.

"You must be the G.A.E.L. team. I'm Mila Winters." She held out a hand to the tall thin man who stepped forward.

He took her hand, shaking it once before returning it to the rifle butt strapped across his chest. "Good to meet you, Dr. Winters. I'm Carl, the team's lead." He pointed to a pink-haired elf with a large pack on her back and several grenades strapped to her chest under her rifle. "This is Jenny, our demo expert."

The pink-haired elf tipped her black helmet like it was a cap. "Nice to meet you, Dr. Winters," she said, shaking Mila's hand.

Carl hiked a thumb over his shoulder to a huge orc, who was surprisingly not equipped with a weapon besides a pistol in a thigh holster. "This is Howard, our front-line caster. He's quick with the spells, and can rip a guy's arms off if they get too close."

Howard rolled his eyes, and in a very clear voice that

spoke of education and proper decorum, said, "I would never rip a man's arms off. Far too messy. A pleasure."

They shook hands, and Mila was about to ask him something when Carl continued,

"This rogue is Nick." He pointed out a gaunt dark-haired Peabrain who flashed a smile through his five o'clock shadow and reached out a hand, which Mila took.

"Dr. Winters." He nodded. "I'm front-line melee and scouting."

Mila looked him over and noted he had no weapons, not even the tactical bulletproof vest. He was wearing a black shirt and trousers and black combat boots.

"Looks like you forgot your gear, Nick."

He chuckled but Carl was the one to answer, rubbing his solid chin as he considered the dark-haired man. "Nick specializes in form-changing, usually bears and the like for fights and weasels and cats for scouting. It's a damn handy set of skills." Nick gave a lazy salute at the compliment.

"That'll be helpful. One of the big problems with the Rougarou is how fucking big they are," Danica said, coming over and wiping her hands on a bar towel.

Mila nodded. "They're a good eight feet tall."

Carl nodded. "We've fought them before. Nasty sons of bitches." A small woman stepped out from behind Carl.

She was shorter than Mila by a good two inches, which made Mila's eyes widen. At 4'10" she hardly ever met a grown adult who was shorter than her.

"Oh, I'm sorry," Mila apologized, not realizing the introductions were not over. "I didn't see you standing behind Carl." She reached out a hand and the small woman took it, shaking with a fairly weak grip.

She looked human, but Mila spotted the wand tucked into a holster beside her only other weapon, a pistol in a thigh holster, which said she was more than likely a witch. She nodded, making the slightly large helmet wobble on her brown hair, which had been twisted into a tight bun at the nape of her neck.

"This is Tina," Carl said, nodding at the small woman. "She doesn't talk much, but when she does, it's filthy."

Tina gave him a withering look, but the others on the team burst out laughing.

"Sorry, Tina." Carl chuckled. "Just have to bust on the new guy. Tina here is our artillery and utility witch. She's in charge of things like crowd control and long-range targets."

"Glad to meet you all. Please just call me Mila. Dr. Winters takes too long," Mila said with a smile, turning to introduce her two companions. "This is Danica Meadows. She's a medical doctor and healer. And this is Harvey, the mayor of Elk River and the bartender here at the Red Brick Tavern."

Everyone exchanged handshakes before they seated themselves at the largest table in the bar, a huge round wooden thing with seats enough for twelve.

"We're still waiting for Penny to get back," Mila informed them. "She's following the Rougarou and will be able to let us know where we need to go. Can't do anything until then. We were just fortifying what we could in case the wolfmen came back."

Carl nodded. "Good idea. Do you mind if we see if there's anything we can add?"

"That would be great," Harvey said, standing up and

pointing to the back of the bar. "The back door in particular could use a little love."

Carl signaled for Tina and Howard to go with him. "See if you can do something about the structure while you're at it," he said as Tina passed him and gave a nod.

"What's wrong with the structure?" Mila asked when they were gone.

"Nothing, I'm sure, but it's just a wooden building," Carl said, waving a hand to indicate the plaster walls. "Most people don't realize the walls of a structure are usually just siding, some kind of insulation, and plaster on the inside. If you're lucky, code requires a layer of plywood in there somewhere, but on something this old?" He shook his head. "I'll eat my helmet if there's even insulation. Howard and Tina can reinforce it with spells they mastered for just such an occasion."

"I didn't realize the walls were such an easy way into a building," Mila said, eying the walls suspiciously.

Carl waved it away. "Most modern buildings are much safer, but you have to watch out for the old ones. If we don't prepare, a Rougarou could just charge through a wall without even feeling it. Don't worry about it; they can take care of it." He leaned on the table, resting an elbow on the worn surface. "Preston gave us the basic rundown, but if we're waiting for your dragon friend to return anyway, why don't you start from the top?"

Mila cocked her head and narrowed her eyes. "How did you know Penny is a dragon?"

Carl chuckled along with the rest of his team. "Mila, we've met before."

Her eyes went wide. How had she forgotten meeting

these people? Was her journey into Valkyriehood messing with her memories? "I'm sorry, I don't remember."

"Let me rephrase that," Carl amended when he saw the distress in her eyes. "We were one of the teams that fought with you against the Dark Star. All of us but Tina; she hadn't joined up yet. We never officially met, but after the battle, we did say hello in passing. I caught glimpses of the fight forming on my side of the park. Plus, when a dwarf king and a dragon show up on Earth, people start talking. Not to mention, you showed some impressive powers out there." He held up a hand, forestalling her comment. "We know what you are because information is power, and Preston likes his teams to be informed before they get into combat. But also know that that information stops with my team. Your secret is safe with us."

Mila felt uncomfortable with how many people knew she was a Valkyrie, but to be fair, most of them found out before she had been told by Victoria to keep it a secret. Besides, the G.A.E.L. team would have found out soon enough fighting beside her. Or at the very least, they would know something was weird about her magic.

"I appreciate that. What should I call you? Sergeant? Lieutenant?" Her face flushed with embarrassment. "Sorry, I don't know much about the military."

He smiled. "We don't have a rank system beyond what we use internally in case a new team lead needs to take over in the field. We're a private organization that doesn't operate beyond the squad formation. Formal rank isn't needed. You can just call me Carl."

"Carl, right. So, this is what we're working with?"

Mila told him everything she could think of, including

the part about Heather since they already knew she was a Valkyrie and the info would do nothing but help the situation. After he had all the details, Carl sat back in his chair, his thumb and bent forefinger stroking his shaved chin.

"Can you handle the magic-user?" he asked, an eyebrow rising.

Mila thought about it and nodded. "I think so. The three of us should be able to handle her. What are you thinking?"

"Divide and conquer."

"What about this Lord of hers?" Mila asked.

"She said he was still slumbering, right? I'm guessing that means he's not going to be much of a threat, but we can reassess when we see the battleground."

The front door opened, and as one, everyone at the table stood and readied either weapons or spells, pointing them at the intruder.

Penny's eyes went wide, and she threw her hands up in surrender.

Everyone relaxed and stowed weapons and spells.

"Chi chi," Penny said, her hands still up.

Mila rolled her eyes. "Yeah, we know it's you. Were you able to track them?"

Penny smiled and launched herself toward the table, flapping her wings once before landing. "Shir shee shee. Chi shir?"

Mila got up and went behind the bar, grabbing a bag of chips and a sleeve of cookies from the rack and brought them back, tossing the snacks to Penny. The dragon snatched the chips, and tore the bag open, shoveling chips into her mouth like the Cookie Monster, sending shards raining down.

"She needs to replenish her magic. We skipped lunch," Mila explained. "She said they went back to the sawmill. Evidently they didn't even try to not be seen, just tore a path directly there."

"Are they inside or out?" Carl asked Penny, who had finished with the chips in record time and was tearing the cookies open.

Her mouth was still full of chips, and she held up a finger while she chewed quickly before swallowing the mouthful. "Shir squee."

"Inside," Mila translated. "She couldn't get a good view of what was happening in there since they closed the big overhead doors before she could get close."

Nick barked a laugh. "You got all that from two words?"

Mila shrugged. "More or less. I edited out a lot of the swearing. Didn't want to offend your delicate ears."

Jenny elbowed Nick in the ribs, laughing. "Man, she's going to fit right in."

"Oh, come on. She couldn't have said anything too bad. Look how cute she is. I could tickle dat widdle belly for hours," Nick said, descending into cutesy baby talk as he made tickling motions with his fingers.

Penny stopped mid-chew, slowly swiveling her head to give him a deathly stare. She spat out her mouthful of cookies before bursting into a very long rant that included several jets of flame and a number of hand gestures that needed no translation.

When she finished, she pulled out a fresh cookie and bit it in half while staring Nick down.

He swallowed hard before slowly turning to Mila, who just smiled. "What did she say?"

"She said she would appreciate it if you didn't demean her as if she were a pet. She is easily the most intelligent person in a hundred miles, and would appreciate if you treated her as such," Mila translated, the smile never leaving her face.

Nick swallowed. "She was talking for a while there. That's all she said?"

Mila shrugged. "More or less."

CHAPTER FIFTEEN

Danica teleported Carl and Howard to the outskirts of the sawmill to show them where it was, then quickly brought them back to the bar.

Mila told Harvey that they shouldn't be long and to expect his people to arrive en masse, then to set up the front door barricade and wait for her and the G.A.E.L. team to return by teleport. He wished them luck and shook her hand.

"Be careful."

She smiled. "One day, people won't feel the need to tell me that all the time. Don't worry, Harvey. I'm much tougher than I look."

They prepared their weapons, and Mila activated her armor. She gave Carl the signal that she, Danica, and Penny were ready, and they all teleported to the location Danica had shown them.

The three large bubbles popped, depositing them behind a fallen tree, thick with underbrush. The G.A.E.L.

team immediately fell into a defensive posture, scanning the area for any signs of the enemy. Carl gave the all-clear signal, and they quietly moved up the edge of the woods overlooking the clearing with the sawmill and derelict buildings.

Crouching in the underbrush, Carl held up a hand, forming a grapefruit-sized bubble from the dim light in his palm. A sharp smell like cut grass hit Mila's nostrils as she watched the first bubble float up a few feet and a second one form in his hand. After a second, the two bubbles glowed and pulsed for a few beats before the floating bubble became so clear she could barely make it out against the sky. The bubble still in Carl's hand, however, showed a slightly shifted view.

The floating bubble rose quickly, climbing past the tall cedar trees that surrounded them. Mila's jaw dropped when she saw the view in the stationary bubble climb along with the other bubble.

"Holy shit," Mila whispered. "It's like a camera drone."

Penny, perched on her shoulder, nodded in appreciation. "Chi."

Once the bubble drone was above the trees, it moved forward quickly. Mila watched as it made a circular route around the large green metal sawmill; it would zoom in the view at some unspoken command from Carl, inspecting potential ingress points before moving on to find more. When the entire building had been viewed from afar, Carl moved in closer, confident there were no lookouts on guard. He got in close to a few windows but found that they were all painted black from the inside.

He spent a good ten minutes looking for any kind of opening to get a look inside but to no avail.

"Fuck," he grumbled, reminding Mila of Finn for a second.

"Looks pretty sealed up," Mila said. "Guess they don't want anyone seeing what's going on."

"Shir shee shee," Penny suggested.

Mila nodded. "Could be. Maybe this Lord of hers is sensitive to light."

"Or it could just be that she doesn't want anyone seeing what's going on. Either way, we need to get an idea of what's going on in there." Carl licked his lips as he stared across the clearing in consideration. He banished the bubble drone with a shake of his hand. "Nick. You're up."

Mila glanced over and saw Nick give a sharp nod, his perpetual half-smile gone and replaced by a thin-lipped determination. Closing his eyes, he formed a bubble between his hands about the size of a basketball. The scent of rosemary filtered through the breeze as he brought the bubble to his face and let it cling to his skin, molding to every nook and cranny. He pulled his hands away, and the bubble continued to crawl across his face, expanding down his neck, then shoulders.

After a few seconds, it covered him from head to toe, leaving a rainbow sheen across his skin and clothes. In less than a second, he shrank and disappeared into the underbrush. There was a popping sound, then the black head of a weasel rose above the ground cover and snapped a sharp salute before scurrying toward the large green metal building.

"Now we wait," Howard said in a deep rumbling bass.

Mila settled onto her knees, trying to keep track of Nick. He was darting from cover to cover just like a real weasel would. His movements were spot on, speaking to the time he put into his particular specialty.

Even knowing what to look for, Mila lost sight of Nick several times. She watched him dart into an outbuilding and expected him to emerge on the other side of the half-collapsed building, but he never did. She was about to mention that she had lost him when Penny pointed from her shoulder. She followed the talon and saw the small black form at the corner of the main building. He sniffed the ground for a second, then sprinted to a section of the corrugated green metal where a couple of rivets had come loose, and quick as a whip, he was through the hole.

"I have to say, that was impressive," Mila whispered. "He didn't give himself away in the least."

"He spends a lot of time in weasel form," Howard said, pulling a toothpick from one of the pockets on his vest and gently putting it between his teeth.

"Why?" Danica asked as she counted her remaining arrows. She frowned. "Fourteen. I should have gotten more from the house."

Howard reached out a large green hand. "Let me see one of those arrows if you don't mind, Dr. Meadows."

She slipped one out of her belt quiver and handed it over. "You can just call me Danica."

He took the arrow and inspected it closely. "Thank you, Danica. To answer your question, he spends so much time as a weasel because he says it saves on food costs. He's saving to buy an airplane. I don't know why since he can teleport with a high level of accuracy."

"It's because he likes planes, Howie," Jenny said, rolling her eyes. "Just because it ain't efficient, don't mean it ain't fun."

Howard handed the arrow back to Danica. "Thank you. How many more would you like?"

Danica's brows went up in surprise. "Oh, uh, sixteen?"

Howard nodded, a smile forming over the tusks jutting from his lower jaw. "An even thirty. That's a good number. Give me a few minutes."

He held out his hands, pressing his thumb and forefinger together like he was pinching something, then touched the pinched fingers together and slowly pulled them apart. As his fingers drew apart, a long thin bubble formed between his fingers. When it was the length of one of Danica's arrows, he released his fingers and the bubble popped, a perfect replica of her arrow dropping into his lap. He repeated the process, producing another perfect replica.

"Well, that's impressive," Mila said.

"Tell me about it," Danica said in awe. "Do you have any idea the level of concentration it takes to remember every detail of something as you replicate it? That's some top-level magic right there."

They watched Howard creating arrows for a few minutes before Mila noticed Danica nervously picking at her artificial hand and staring off into the distance.

She leaned over and shoulder-bumped her friend. "What's wrong?"

She smiled a sad smile. "Oh, nothing important. I was just thinking about Phil."

Mila frowned, reaching over and taking Danica's hand in hers, keeping her from picking at the diamond construct. "It seems pretty important. I mean we're about to storm the castle and your thinking about your boyfriend. What's up? Are you worried you're going to get hurt again?"

Danica shook her head emphatically. "No, it's not that. I've just been thinking that I need to make a decision soon about us."

"Like deciding to stay together? I thought you two were getting along great. I know Finn really likes him, and he tends to be a pretty good judge of character."

Penny chuckled, making Mila give her side-eye. Penny looked away, obviously avoiding eye contact.

"We are getting along great. That's kind of the problem." She plucked a blade of long grass out of the ground, and absent-mindedly wound it between her fingers. "I could see myself with him long-term. Like marrying him, long-term."

Mila grinned. "I don't see the problem. That's great news."

"Yeah, except that I'm an elf and he's a Peabrain. Not to mention that he doesn't know about any of this," she said, holding up her magical prosthetic.

"Oh, right. I forget he doesn't know about magic." Mila bit her lip. "What are you thinking? Are you going to tell him or keep it a secret? It's not like he's going to see through your concealment spells. I mean, I lived with you for more than ten years and had no idea you were an elf."

"Yeah, I could do that, but eventually, he would get that something was up. If we got married, twenty years from now he's going to be in his fifties, and I'll still look like this. He's not dumb, so he would figure out that something was up."

Mila nodded. "What other option is there?"

"I could tell him," Danica said, tossing the blade of grass away.

"That might not be so bad. I took it pretty well. Who's to say he wouldn't too?"

"Yeah, but if he doesn't, then I would have to get Hermin to erase his memories, and that can lead to all sorts of problems. Either way, I end up losing him."

"Unless he just accepts it." Mila chuckled. "He is a bit of a nerd. He would probably eat this shit up."

Danica laughed. "I suppose that's true. I just don't want to lose him. The choices are, tell him now and maybe lose him, or wait and lose him after decades of marriage."

"Can't you just tell him, and if it doesn't work out, have Hermin erase his memories and continue on like nothing happened?"

She shook her head. "Having me around would make the memories resurface. If he doesn't accept the magical world, we would have to erase everything with me. The brain is a really hard thing to trick for too long."

"It's true," Carl said, making Mila jump. She hadn't realized he was listening. "Same thing happened with my ex. Told her, and she didn't know how to handle it."

"What happened?" Mila asked.

He gave her a sad smile. "That's why she's my ex." He

looked back at the sawmill. "Nick's out. Get ready to move."

Mila saw the black weasel running full out for the edge of the forest. She wasn't very familiar with weasel expressions, but the one on his face was unmistakable.

He was freaking out.

CHAPTER SIXTEEN

Nick didn't even take the time to transform back into a human before he began reporting. It was odd to see a foot-long weasel speaking, especially since his normal tenor was several octaves higher due to the small size. He had climbed up onto a fallen branch to get out of the underbrush and sat on his haunches, wringing his hands in a very weasel-like way.

"She was right, Carl. I counted thirty-two Rougarou. These bastards are fuckin huge, too. Probably twenty percent bigger than the ones we took care of in Baton Rouge, and more intelligent. Not smart, but I would call them well-trained."

Carl's face was hard and thin-lipped as he listened to the report. "What about the caster?"

Nick nodded his furry head. "She's a witch, but she was calling up some real bad juju in there. Nothing like she should be able to do. Not particularly powerful, but it was strange and didn't taste right. Spouting off some crazy shit about the return of Azoth, and how her dreams have led them so far and blah blah. The usual word vomit from her kind.

"She was in a back area that's been sectioned off with big black curtains. I counted five cages with the townsfolk in em back there. The girl Heather was there too, chained up with a magic suppressing collar. She wasn't looking so good," he said, giving Mila an apologetic look. "The room was a classic altar setup—a big fucking statue of some guy in a stone throne behind a stone slab. It was pretty obvious the altar had been used before. I'm guessing that's where they made all the Rougarou.

"When I approached the cages, I felt the pull of magic on me. I'm pretty sure the iron in the cages is anti-magic as well. I didn't want to get too close in case it forced me to change back."

Carl was quiet for a few seconds, rubbing his chin in thought as they all waited for him to formulate a plan. He glanced at Jenny, his blue eyes cold. "Jenny, head in that direction," he pointed to the north of the dirt road that led to the sawmill, "and start setting up the usual traps. Keep the explosives small enough that we don't start too many fires. Remember, we'll need to clean up when we're done."

Jenny nodded, hiking her heavy pack higher on her shoulders before moving out with the unnatural stealth only an elf in the woods could accomplish. The evil grin on her face was all Mila needed to see to know just how much she enjoyed her job.

"Nick, we're going to need to pull those Rougarou out, can you rip one of the overhead doors off and bait them into chasing you?"

Nick nodded. "Yeah, they're trained, but they still think like a pack of wolves. I'll give em something to chase."

"Good, this is going to be a classic pull and hold action. Tina, head after Jenny and set yourself up with a good vantage. I'm going to want you out of reach but still able to tangle those wolfmen up. We need to buy time for Mila and Danica to do their thing."

Tina nodded and stood, but Howard put a hand on her arm, forestalling her. "Carl, I believe the combo Tina and I pulled off with that Wendigo last week would work well with the Rougarou's large numbers."

Carl nodded. "Good call, Howard. Entangle and acid spray are a good combo for these things. Try to keep the acid off the trees; the last thing we need is the Huldus complaining to Preston. Go, and I'll be along in a minute."

The huge orc and the tiny witch crouch-ran in the direction of their teammates.

"Are you sure you can handle the witch?" Carl asked, not unsure, just giving Mila the chance to make an informed decision after Nick's report.

"It shouldn't be a problem. If it gets too hairy, Danica can always teleport us out, and we can come back when we're better prepared."

Carl nodded, opening a flap on his vest and pulling out a small plastic box. He popped it open to reveal four in-ear comm units. He handed two to Mila and Danica. "Sorry, Penny. I don't have any small enough for you."

Penny shrugged, used to the idea that most of the tech on Earth was made for Peabrains.

When they had the comms in their ears, Carl did a quick test, and the girls gave him a thumbs-up. "Okay, if you need to contact the team, just press the button on the earpiece and talk."

"Got it. When do we go?" Mila asked, pulling out her Ivar.

"As soon as Nick is ready," he said, pointing over Mila's shoulder.

She turned and saw that the weasel had coated himself in another bubble. This time he grew in size. Then he kept on growing. Mila had to tilt her head back to see the top of the multicolored bubble with an amorphous furry shape inside it.

With a quiet pop, the bubble vanished, leaving the largest bear Mila had ever seen. Nick had transformed into a grizzly bear that stood nearly eighteen feet tall on his back legs. His massive head swiveled around and grinned at Mila, making the animal part of her brain scream in terror as she fought to keep from scooting back.

Nick dropped to all fours, and Mila noted that he was still taller than her at the shoulder by at least a foot.

"Ready," he growled in a deep rumbling voice. "We need to get this going before she starts sacrificing people."

Carl put a finger to his ear, pressing the call button. "How are we on preparations?"

Mila heard the other three report that they were ready.

Carl gave Nick a nod. "You're a go, Nick."

The great lumbering figure of Grizzly Nick stepped out into the clearing and started galloping. Watching the huge mass of the bear pick up speed was awe-inspiring. He seemed to glide over the clearing, each step eating up a dozen feet or more. Before she knew it, Nick reared up on his back legs in front of the large metal overhead door, his massive paws outstretched overhead, claws gleaming in the afternoon sun.

A roar that shook dead branches of the surrounding trees exploded from his maw as he tore down with his paws. The thin metal of the door gave way under the sharp claws, and he used his massive weight to rip a hole in the door large enough for him to enter without a problem. He roared again, charging into the darkness.

Mila swallowed and forced herself to breathe. She had never seen such ferocity from anyone but Finn, and Nick's massive size added to the terror.

Yelps and barking filtered out of the building along with more roars from Nick.

There were a few seconds of relative silence, then the broken body of a Rougarou flew out one of the black-paned windows, shattering the glass and sending the body ten feet out into the clearing. Another dead Rougarou was flung through the opening in the door, tumbling into a bloody heap and not moving.

A black and purple bolt of destructive energy shot out of the opening, followed by another in quick secession.

"Get out of there, Nick. You can't stand up against that kind of magic," Carl said calmly.

A few seconds later, the great bear shot out of the door at a full run. Right on his heels, black-furred Rougarou began to pour out after him. Nick picked up speed, keeping the wolfmen just out of reach as he led them toward his teammates and the traps lying in wait.

As the last Rougarou left the sawmill, a small figure with red hair in a long black coat stepped out into the light. She watched the retreating pack, then scanned the area with narrow eyes before moving back into the building.

"That's my cue. I'm heading over to flank the Rougarou. You three are up. Kick some ass, and don't be afraid to tele-port out if it gets too hairy. We can always come back later." He gave them a nod, then took off at a run in the direction the pack had vanished.

"Okay, let's do this," Mila said, steeling herself.

She gripped her Ivar tight and made sure the safety was off before jumping to her feet and taking off at a full sprint. She wanted to get to the structure as quickly as possible and find cover.

The clearing was a good hundred yards from the woods to the building, and Mila felt like she ate up the distance quicker than she felt was possible as her adrenaline gave her an extra boost.

She slid to a stop beside the opening in the metal door Nick had made, keeping herself from slamming into the metal and announcing their presence. She glanced back and saw that Danica was right on her heels, and Penny was hovering just behind her.

Focusing on the opening, she leaned in and quickly peeked inside, but there was no one in the large open space. She motioned for the others to follow and quick-stepped through the opening and over to three old fifty-five-gallon drums, using them for cover. Danica and Penny were right behind her, and Danica crouched beside her.

"What do you think?" Danica asked in a quiet voice. "Looks like all the Rougarou followed Nick."

Mila nodded, taking in the room.

The machinery had been removed, leaving a large open

three-story garage-like structure. Dim lighting hung from the ceiling in single bulb lamps, illuminating a set of catwalks on either side of the room and an office on the right upper floor. Everything was covered in dust, grease, and rust. Though the rust-colored stains on the concrete in the center of the room were more than likely blood.

Thick black curtains hung from the ceiling, cutting the room in half and blocking all view of what was on the other side.

"Penny, can you get in there and see if there's a place we can sneak in? The last thing I want to do is pull back the curtain and announce our entrance."

Penny nodded and shot up toward the ceiling where the curtain left gaps she could get through easily. After a few seconds, she reappeared and quickly flew to them.

"Chi! Shir shee." She waved for them to follow and headed for the right side of the curtain.

"Oh, fuck," Mila said, taking off after Penny. "She already has someone on the altar. We need to hurry."

Penny led them to a gap in the curtains in the shadow of the catwalk, and Mila quickly stepped through. Surprisingly the area behind the curtain wasn't in complete darkness like Mila had feared but was still dimly lit, to the point that it took a few seconds for her vision to adapt.

On the other side of the room were the five cages with the townsfolk in them. They were crying and consoling one another, but their movements were sluggish. Mila guessed the enchanted cages were sapping their energy, keeping them docile and relatively quiet.

In the center of the room, suspended from two long chains attached to the ceiling, was Heather, her body held up by the chains around her wrists. Mila could see the black metal collar around her neck, her messy black hair matted and full of leaves and twigs as if she had been dragged through the forest to get here. Standing in front of a stone altar was the black-clad redheaded witch.

She had her wand out, tracing complicated patterns in the air over the prone form of an elvish woman who being restrained by glowing magical energies around her wrists and ankles. Behind the altar was a figure in a deep hooded robe slumped in a stone throne.

As far as statues went, it was an odd position to put the subject in, but the robe was obviously made of the same stone as the throne, or at least something strikingly similar.

"Lord Azoth! Your servant Seline has brought you another supplicant. Partake unto yourself their power that you might live again," she screamed with a high-pitched fervor that made the hairs on Mila's neck stand on end.

There was no apparent dagger or implement of death you might find at a sacrifice, but Mila didn't want to take any chances. She checked the room quickly for any remaining Rougarou, but they were alone.

"Penny, can you free the townspeople? Melt the locks on the cages or something?"

Penny nodded. "Shee shir."

"That's fine I'll cause a big enough distraction in a minute," Mila reassured her. "Danica, stay behind me, and use me for cover. I don't want you over here out of reach. We need to stay close in case this goes badly."

Penny flew across the room to the cages and hid in the shadows, giving them a thumbs-up to say that she was set.

"Ready," Danica said, nocking an arrow.

Just as Mila was about to move, the elf woman on the altar began to scream as a thin line of blue light rose from her chest and wormed its way into the hood of the statue's figure.

The statue breathed in the light, its shoulders rising and chest expanding.

"I don't think that's a statue," Danica whispered, an edge of fear in her voice.

Mila was frozen with horror. She had seen a wisp of light coming from someone like that before. It had been when she used the Reaper on the Dark Star and pulled out her soul in order to cleanse the darkness from it.

That thing on the throne had just consumed the elf woman's soul.

The body still screamed and convulsed, but the pain that had been there before was gone, and now the sound was hollow, bordering on a howl. As they watched, the ribs expanded with a loud popping crunch. The arms twisted and elongated along with the legs and feet. Her face strained, and her nose and mouth began to push up into a muzzle as tufts of black and gray fur began to rapidly grow on her skin in patches.

"Fucking hell," Danica whispered in horror.

That simple curse snapped Mila out of her daze. She raised her pistol and pulled the trigger.

CHAPTER SEVENTEEN

A spear of pure raw celestial magic exploded from the barrel of the Ivar and streaked across the room, headed for Seline's exposed back. It was a perfect shot, aimed directly at the heart.

Mila smiled; this was going to be easier than she had feared.

Her face fell, however, when from the corner of her eye, she saw the figure on the throne lift a hand and power flow from it.

A black mist formed behind the unsuspecting witch, swirling into a wall of black and purple magic. The bolt from Mila's Ivar slammed into it, causing a shower of gold and purple sparks before both magics consumed each other, vanishing to nothingness.

Seline spun, her red pigtails flaring out from her head, her eyes wide with surprise. "My Lord!" she squeaked in surprise, her childlike voice making Mila uncomfortable with how out of place it was. "You saved your wretched servant's life. I am beyond thankful." Her face fell, and she grinned evilly at Mila and Danica behind her. She continued in a deeper voice, "I shall prove my worth, Lord Azoth."

She raised her wand and shot off a ball of the dark mist, followed by another, then a third in quick secession.

Mila raised her arm just in time, her shield forming an instant before the smoking orbs slammed into it.

Mila was still feeding the shield when the first orb hit, and she was immediately thankful she was. The orb burst, splashing a black and purple viscous liquid across its golden surface and began to eat through the magical construct. The only reason the second and third orbs didn't break through was that she was continually rein-forcing the magic that was being sucked away.

The effort to keep the shield up was taxing, but Mila pushed the mounting headache out of her mind and took aim with the Ivar.

She let off another shot, making the pain in her head to jump several notches as more power was demanded from her.

The bolt slammed into another wall of mist, but this one was of Seline's making. The sudden shocking drain on her made the witch stumble back a few steps, clutching the side of her head with her free hand, to Mila's great delight.

The rattling of chains drew Mila's attention to Heather, who had spun to look at Mila. They locked eyes, and Heather's went wide.

"You need to get out of here!" she croaked, her voice raspy and raw.

Danica let several arrows loose, making Seline have to

defend herself from the incoming missiles, which she did by batting them away with unnatural speed.

"We're here to save you and the others," Mila said with a jerk of her head toward the cages.

Penny hovered a few feet from a large padlock holding the first cage's door in place, blowing a concentrated jet of flame over it. The metal was glowing bright orange and beginning to droop.

Danica continued to fire arrows, but it seemed to be no more than a distraction to Seline, who raised her wand and sent out another barrage of smoking black orbs. Mila focused on the fight, missing what Heather said as the orbs slammed into her shield, drawing even more power this time.

Mila returned fire, this time sending two shots at Seline, who blocked them with a hastily constructed wall of dark magic. She didn't flinch nearly as much the second time around, instead pointing her wand at Mila and releasing a torrent of the black and purple magic at Mila's shield.

The substance clung to the shield, eating away at it faster than Mila could replenish it. Black and gold sparks flew as the two magics fought for dominance. Mila began to feel weak at the knees as her power was sucked away at a prodigious rate.

A hole appeared in the shield, dripping black magic onto her leg. There was no pain, but a sizzling black smoke rose up from the drop. Mila quickly adjusted her stance to avoid the leak and poured even more power into the shield.

She was vaguely aware of Danica firing arrows as fast

as she could from behind her, but as far as Mila could tell, it wasn't doing much good. The arrows were either being evaporated in the stream of magic, or Seline was smacking them away, but it was distracting her a little.

Mila fought off the nausea that was creeping in and took a quick shot with the Ivar, this time aiming at Seline's legs. She fired the shot from the bottom of her shield, hoping that the witch's continual stream of black magic would block her view of the incoming bolt until it was too late.

The golden spear of magic streaked across the ground, closing the distance in a flash. Seline saw the incoming projectile, but it was too late. She cut off the flow of magic and tried to get a wall up, but the bolt slammed into her legs just below the knee and exploded in a shower of golden sparks.

Seline was thrown into the air, tumbling end over end past the throne and slamming into the wall hard enough that the lights began to sway on their long cords, making the shadows dance.

Mila lowered her shield, letting her power replenish. The figure on the throne hadn't moved since the beginning of the fight, but the elf woman had continued the painful transformation and was now a fully formed Rougarou. However, she was still held to the altar by the magical restraints. That didn't keep her from thrashing around and gnashing her teeth impotently.

Mila rushed to Heather, reaching out to take the shackles off.

"Don't," she moaned.

Mila ignored her and grabbed the cuff on Heather's

right wrist. Mila felt a pull on her power that almost made her faint after expending as much as she had in the battle.

"I told you," Heather said, her eyes heavy. "You can't remove them without draining your power."

Mila glanced over Heather's shoulder and saw that Penny was on the third cage, the first two empty. Obviously, the townsfolk didn't need to be told to get the hell out of there.

"How do I save you?" Mila asked, desperation in her voice. She shook the Valkyrie when she didn't respond. "Heather! How do I free you?"

She looked into Mila's eyes. "You can't, little sister. It would take far too long. You have to take a message to Victoria. Tell her the Drude is alive. It's coming for us all. Remember that. The Drude. Now go. You have to get out of here and get the message to the sisterhood. They will know what to do."

"I'm not leaving you here," Mila argued, trying to think of a way to get the shackles off but coming up empty.

"Don't worry, little sister. I'm not as weak as I appear. I still have a few tricks up my sleeve. But your presence is draining me far too much. I need you to put distance between us before my powers are completely gone."

Mila opened her mouth to protest, but Heather was right. Mila was too weak to break the shackles, and her presence as a Lone Valkyrie was eating away at what powers Heather had left.

Grinding her teeth, Mila refused to believe there was nothing she could do. Then her eyes went wide as she realized there *was* something she could do. She reached into her pocket and pulled out her sisterhood phone, hitting the power button, but it wouldn't turn on. She hit the button again, but nothing. Flipping the phone over, she saw a circular hole melted into the back where the dark magic had dripped onto it when her shield had failed.

"Come on!" Mila growled. "Fucking motherfucker! This is some grade-A bullshit."

Heather began to laugh hoarsely. "Sometimes life isn't fair, little one. In fact, it rarely is."

The sound of heavy footfalls made Mila spin just in time to see the Rougarou from the altar swing its massive hand full of razor-sharp talons into her chest.

She heard Danica scream something as the wind was knocked from her lungs and she was tossed across the room from the impact.

Mila was glad to see that Penny had moved to the last cage, and there was a group of people scrambling for the exit from the previous cage. Penny was doing good work.

Then Mila hit something hard and blacked out.

CHAPTER EIGHTEEN

M ila sucked in a breath of air, sitting up on the concrete floor of the sawmill. She rubbed her head for a second, trying to remember what she was supposed to be doing. She looked around for a clue.

Danica was quickly stepping back, putting arrow after arrow into a charging Rougarou.

The haze was banished from Mila's mind in an instant. She climbed to her feet and sprinted at the Rougarou. Reaching behind her and pulling out Gram, she whispered the power word, unfolding the sword as she swung it. It flashed with a golden light, completing its transformation from a handle to a gold longsword just as it bit into the charging beast's midsection.

Mila screamed with rage, driving the sword in a sweeping arc. The razor's edge passed through flesh like it wasn't even there, and when the blade hit the spine, Mila summoned a strength she didn't know she possessed and drove it through the bone. It came out the wolfman's back, and both halves slid to the floor.

Mila stood, legs apart, sword dripping blood, as she sucked in a deep breath.

The last lock fell to the floor, drawing Mila's attention. She watched as the frightened magicals pushed their way out of the cell and ran for the relative safety of the town.

Mila awkwardly pressed the call button on her earpiece with a finger on the hand that still held the Ivar. "Carl, the last of the captives are free. You need to cover them as long as you can. Keep those pups busy."

"No problem," came Carl's short reply.

A shrill whistle made everyone in the room cringe. Mila was surprised to see Selina walking toward them, a whistle in her lips. She finished the long note, then put the whistle in her coat pocket.

"I have to admit, that was a lot of fun," Seline said with girlish glee. "I haven't had a challenge like you in a while."

Carl cut into her earpiece. "The Rougarou have broken off and are returning to the sawmill. You need to get out of there. There are at least twenty of the bastards left."

Mila reached up and hit the button to reply, ignoring Selina while keeping an eye on her. "Can you pursue? We need to kill them all."

"We can try, but the motherfuckers are fast."

"Do your best," Mila said, dropping the pistol to her side.

"It's rude to ignore your host," Selina said with a frown. She pointed an accusing finger at the empty cages. "Look what you did. Now I have to go get more food for Lord Azoth."

"You and your sleepy buddy back there are not going to be doing anything. The jig's up, Seline," Mila said, angry that she couldn't really see how she was going to back that statement up.

Seline didn't either if her giggling was any indication. "I liked the trick with the bear, but my Rougarou are on their way back, and when they get here, they are going to rip your arms off and eat them for a snack," she said, excitedly clapping her hands.

"You have got something seriously wrong with you," Mila said, disgust on her face. "You know that, right?"

Seline's face became twisted with hate. "My Lord says I'm special. Are you calling him a liar?"

Mila pointed to Azoth still in the same position he was the last time she looked. "Him? Yeah, he's lying to you. You're not special, you're weak. That's how he controls you —through your weakness."

Seline stomped her foot like a toddler and stared daggers at Mila. Then without any warning, she whipped her wand out and pointed it at Mila.

Heather suddenly growled with effort and began to glow with golden light. Shimmering wings of light began to appear as her growl turned into a yell of effort. She was standing now, not slack in her bonds. She turned her face to Azoth, rage and anger plain on her face.

"You wanted a Valkyrie? Well, now you have one." Heather's voice was strong and clear.

Her wings became solid, their plumage sharp geometric lines that looked more like golden knives than feathers. Mila could feel the power pouring off her in waves. She also knew Heather didn't have that much power left. This was a last-ditch effort on her part, and Mila knew it.

Heather flexed her back, then jerked her right hand

down. The chain strained, then a loud clang sounded from up near the ceiling, and twenty feet of metal came raining down in a pile beside the Valkyrie.

Seline's eyes were wide with fear. She had thought Heather was nothing more than a husk at that point, but clearly, she had been wrong. She took a step backward then another before turning to run.

"Oh, no, you don't," Heather said, slashing her arm back, and the twenty feet of chain along with it, then she snapped the chain forward like a whip.

The heavy chain sailed through the air and wrapped around Seline's waist, pinning one arm to her torso.

Golden light shot down the chain, jumping from link to link until it struck Seline and consumed her.

Seline began to scream, smoke roiling off her as she convulsed under the attack. The amount of power coming off Heather was impressive but unsustainable. Heather didn't seem to care as she started screaming in pain along with Seline.

Mila tried to think of how to stop this, but Heather had made her decision and was obviously going to burn herself out and take Seline with her.

The light traveling down the chain suddenly ceased and Seline slumped to the floor, but Heather continued her tormented wails. Mila didn't understand what was happening at first, then she saw Azoth slowly rise form his throne.

He held out a dark gray hand toward Heather, and Mila saw the strand of her soul come loose and begin to be pulled toward his palm.

"No!" Mila screamed, pointing and firing the Ivar without thought.

The bolts of magic slammed into a barrier he erected with a thought. The barrier and the spears of magic were consumed as he continued to draw the Valkyrie's soul into him.

Mila began to charge forward, but Danica's hand on her shoulder stopped her. "You can't. He'll kill you."

Mila felt a sense of helplessness fall over her as she realized there was nothing she could do. This creature was unbelievably powerful, and it was still half asleep. She needed to get hold of Victoria as soon as possible.

In seconds Heather's screams cut off as the last of the golden light was pulled from her chest and into Azoth. He breathed in deeply, expanding his chest under the gray robe.

"My Lord, that is too much power this early. You need more sustenance before you can eat such a rich meal," Seline mumbled from where she was pushing herself up off the floor.

"There was little left, my child. A perfect amount for my current state." Azoth's voice sounded like a hundred creaking doors being pulled open at once. It was harsh and raspy but still had a deep power to it.

He turned to Heather's unmoving form, face twisted in a frozen expression of pain, and smiled. "Delicious." He reached out and pressed a finger to her forehead.

Mila, Danica, and Penny gasped when her body crumbled to dust, the shackles dropping to the concrete with a resounding clang.

"Take the town. This time do it right, Seline. I require more sacrifice."

Seline bowed low. "As you command, my Lord."

He turned to face Mila. The deep hood hid his features, but the unmistakable feeling of his eyes upon her made her skin crawl.

"You will replace her, young one. You may not have the depth of power your older sister possessed, but you do have a lot of it."

He held out a hand toward her, a dark cloud forming in his palm.

Mila didn't see what happened next. Instead, she felt Danica's hand fall on her shoulder, and they teleported away.

CHAPTER NINETEEN

Mila stumbled forward, catching herself on the large round wooden table in the Red Brick Tavern.

Harvey, who was sitting at the table, jumped up, brandishing a baseball bat and yelling in fright. "Holy fuck, Mila. I think I just shit myself." He leaned hard on the table, taking a couple of gulping breaths.

Mila didn't waste time explaining; instead, she hit the call button on her comm. "Carl. We had to teleport to the bar. The witch is still alive, and she's woken some creature. I think it's still weak, but they are sending the Rougarou to take the town. You need to get back here asap."

Her comm crackled and Carl's voice came through, out of breath from running. "We're already on the way there. The pack outpaced us, but we passed the last group of survivors as they were headed into town. We're escorting them now. We have another couple of miles to go. ETA, twenty minutes."

"Got it. We'll start evacuating people. We can't hold this bar for long against twenty of those things."

"Yeah, about that. Turns out, there was a second pack. When the first pack disengaged, we spotted another large group of the wolfmen moving toward the sawmill. I couldn't get a definite count, but my guess is there are another thirty of the motherfuckers joining up with the rest."

"Great. The hits just keep coming. Get here quick. I have a feeling those Rougarou are going to outpace the survivors pretty quickly."

"My thoughts exactly." Carl cut the comm.

Mila turned to the gathered townsfolk. "Who here can teleport? Raise your hands." Only three people raised their hands, two Peabrain men, and an elven woman. "Great. How many can you take at once?"

"Three," the older of the two Peabrains said, tucking his hands into his into the bib of his denim overalls and resting them on his large round belly.

"I can probably do two, including me," the young man said.

The elven woman looked to be about twenty, but she could have just as easily have met Lincoln in person for all Mila knew. She had an air of rugged confidence about her. "I can do three as well. Where are we going?"

"Well, firstly we're getting you all someplace safe, then we can come back and clean this mess up properly. I own a condo building in Denver that's being converted into housing for magicals. The bottom floor is still open, so we're going to take you all there for now. Danica here will take the three of you there now, then bring you back to start ferrying the rest while we keep the Rougarou busy."

"What happened to the rest of us? Did you save them,

or are they dead too?" the elven woman asked, her eyes narrow with suspicion.

"Sorry, things have been happening really fast," Mila apologized, licking her lips and realizing she was extremely thirsty. "We saved them. They're on their way, and the first group should be here any minute. In fact, we need someone to keep watch."

Two girls with curly brown hair who looked to be about sixteen raised their hands. "I and my sister can do it. We know a few spells to fight off attackers if it comes down to it." Her sister nodded, pulling a wand out of the sleeve of her sweatshirt.

"Okay, just step outside and keep an eye out. Don't go looking for trouble, for fuck's sake. Get back inside as soon as you spot a Rougarou."

They nodded and ran to the front door, pushing it open and letting in a sliver of golden late afternoon light before it closed behind them.

Danica went to the three other teleporters and had them hold hands. After a second of concentration, a large bubble formed around them then popped, leaving empty air.

Mila sighed, the weight of the day hitting her all at once. She swallowed, her throat incredibly dry. Penny flapped over and landed on her shoulder, giving her a compassionate look.

"Chi?"

Mila half-smiled; it was all she could muster. "I'm fine. I just really thought I could save her."

Penny patted her head and nuzzled her temple.

She reached up and squeezed the little dragon's shoulder affectionately. "Thanks, babe. Love you too."

Licking her lips again, she headed for the bar. "Hey, Harvey, I'm going to grab a drink. You okay with that?"

He waved a defeated hand at her. "Sure. Have at it. I have a feeling the bar's not going to be here in the morning anyway."

Mila wanted to say that was crazy talk, but she had to agree with him. Fifty-plus Rougarou were going to make short work of the place.

Penny pointed to a nice bottle of whiskey. "Shir."

Mila read the label. "Good eye, Penny."

Grabbing the bottle and two rocks glasses, Mila poured two full shots and set the bottle down on the bar. Opening a cooler she remembered seeing Coors originals in, she grabbed one of the beers and twisted the top off.

Danica reappeared with the three townsfolk and instructed them to start taking people to the condo, then headed over to Mila, who handed her a beer.

Danica twisted the top off and took a long drink of the ice-cold beer. "Thanks. I needed that. Got another shot glass?"

Mila smiled and poured her a whiskey. Holding her glass up, she clinked it with Danica's, then Penny's, still on the bar top.

"Cheers. Here's to wishing we had the cushy job today instead of Finn."

"Shee," Penny said with an exaggerated eye roll.

"Lucky bastard," Danica agreed, downing the shot in one go.

CHAPTER TWENTY

F inn dove forward, avoiding the spikes that shot from the wall, but the jet of fire from the pillar in the tight corridor caught the back of his shirt on fire. He twisted in the air, landing on his back, and smothering the flame. Lying still, he looked for more of the traps he knew were there.

One of the floor tiles was slightly raised, a sure sign that it was a pressure plate. He crawled forward, avoiding the plate altogether, and was about to congratulate himself on making it all the way through the hundred-meter-long corridor of death with only a singed shirt when his hand landed on a tile that clicked and dropped a few millimeters.

"Fucking hell."

A click at the ceiling made him twist and roll to the wall as a huge bladed pendulum dropped from the ceiling and swung down to graze him across the ribs. He quickly crab-crawled forward when the blade swung the other way, giving him enough time to roll out of the corridor and into a large natural cave.

He checked his side and saw that there were two shallow cuts along his ribs, one from the initial drop, the second from its return swing. The cuts were shallow enough that they hadn't got to the muscle, but they were bleeding pretty well.

Using Fragar, he cut the bottom third of his t-shirt off, then cut two long strips from that, leaving a large portion that he folded into a pad large enough to cover the two cuts. Pressing the t-shirt scrap to his side, he awkwardly tied it into place with the two long strips., making sure to cinch it tight enough that it wouldn't fall off if he had to fight any more of the little ratmen.

He had a healing potion left, having already taken one after he was ambushed by ten of the skulking little rat fuckers and they had stabbed him in the legs. What pissed him off the most wasn't that they got the drop on him, but that they had destroyed his jeans, leaving them in ribbons from the thigh down. He had been forced to cut the dangling bits of denim off or they would get caught on all sorts of things, inevitably getting him killed.

He loved these pants, and they had ruined them. He wished he could find another group of the rat bastards just so he could take his revenge for his murdered 501s.

Now that triage was done, he took a look around to find the next challenge that awaited him and almost burst into song.

The natural cavern he was in soared dozens of feet above him and was chock-full of stalagmites and stalactites. It looked like what everyone thought caves should look like, greens and blues in the stone, dripping water, the smell of earth and minerals, and right in the center of it all was a pile of gold, silver, and jewels that stood fifteen feet high and spilled out across the ground in a thirty-foot circle.

"Holy shit." Finn chuckled.

He had only seen treasure hoards this large maybe twice in his life, and the first one had been a dragon's hoard. Luckily, he had it on good authority that all the dragons had gone extinct on Earth a couple thousand years ago.

He cautiously approached the pile, keeping an eye out for traps and ambushes. There were plenty of nooks and crannies where ratman could hide, but if they were there, they either were waiting for some signal or losing his favorite jeans had made Finn paranoid and the coast was clear.

He made it all the way to the pile and nothing horrible happened to him, letting him relax just a little bit.

He listened for a full minute, trying to pick out the slightest sound that was out of place, but all he heard was the constant dripping of water and the faint slicing sound of the bladed pendulum swinging back and forth. Convinced he was alone in the cavern, he turned to his prize.

There were hundreds of roughcast gold bars stacked in haphazard piles, along with gold and silver coins minted in the same rough fashion spilling out between the stacked bars and forming a dome of wealth. Gems of all sizes and cuts were peppered throughout the precious metals. He marveled at the massive pile. He didn't know what he had done to get so lucky, but he wouldn't have to find another treasure for Penny anytime soon. He could just keep making trips back here and take what he needed. This was a hoard worthy of the biggest dragon in the universe.

Actually, that wasn't true. He knew the biggest dragon in the universe: Sheena Grontel, the Great Wyrm. She had an entire planet covered in treasures as her hoard. She was also large enough to be seen from orbit and could fly through the interstellar void. Not to mention that she could personally channel more magic than the entire Dwarven Empire combined. Yeah, no one ever tried to steal any of that sweet loot.

Finn slipped the heavy-duty backpack from his shoulders and tried to decide where to start. He could probably get two stacks of five bars each, then fill in the leftover space with coins and gems. Then again, maybe just taking coins would be better. Coins were more "hoard-y," in his thinking.

The problem was that he wasn't sure what Penny needed. If it was a value thing, then the gold bars with coins filling in the cracks was the way to go. Most value for space. However, if it was an aesthetic thing, then coins would be more valuable.

Finn stood there for a good ten minutes debating the issue with himself before chuckling with the realization that it didn't matter. He could just come back and get more, so the point was moot.

Deciding that he personally liked the maximum value method most, he went to work.

Setting the large backpack on the ground, he picked out ten gold bars, trying to find ones of similar size and weight. He quickly realized that all the bars had been cast from five different molds, making the sizes easy to choose.

One of the casts had been slightly bigger than the others, making a brick of gold that was relatively rectangular, at about two inches by six inches and an inch thick. Feeling the weight in his hand, he guessed it was about eight and a half pounds per bar.

He began stacking the bricks side by side, making a four-by-six-inch tower of gold in the bottom of the pack. He realized he was off on the number of bars he could get in the pack by nearly a factor of two. He had forgotten how tall the pack was.

When he had a ten-inch-tall tower, he started to worry about the weight ripping the pack open, so he pulled out a nub of purple chalk and began to mark runes all over it. He started with what he thought the weak points might be, like the seams where the shoulder straps attached, but then realized the material of the pack might not stand up to the punishment. With a sigh, he carefully emptied the pack and methodically went about marking every single piece of material and every seam with the dwarven ruin for strength.

When he was done and about to power the runes, he did the math in his head and decided the one rune might not be enough. It was better to be safe than sorry. The last thing he wanted was to be halfway out of the dungeon and have the bag split open, spilling his hard-earned loot in a dangerous area.

He took another ten minutes to double-rune every-thing. Satisfied, he closed his eyes and began to channel power from the earth into the magically fortified chalk.

The runes lit up one by one in quick succession. When all the runes were glowing, he released the powers potential and let it absorb into the runes fully. As soon as they locked in, the chalk transformed into a glossy paint like substance that would take a lot of effort to remove.

He gave the bag a test, gripping either side of the opening and pulling it apart with all his considerable strength. The fabric didn't even strain at his abuse.

Satisfied, he re-stacked the gold bars, and not finding any more of the same cast bars within easy reach, he switched to coins and began dumping them into the bag. He used his hands in a cupping motion like he was getting water from a pool. He had to be careful with his prosthetic hand since it had slenderer fingers than his normal one, even after he had expanded the adjustment on the digits to their maximum. Finn had large hands, even for a dwarf.

He couldn't believe his luck at finding such a huge hoard of treasure. He guessed it had probably been a dragon's hoard before they had gone extinct. The fact that this treasure had been sitting down here for thousands of years and no one had found it was hysterical to Finn. It had taken him just over eight hours to get where he was. Hell, he knew he had found the treasure when he'd found that first massive room. At that point, it was just a matter of traversing the dungeon.

The bag was nearly full, the bars well-buried at this point. And he had made a nice divot in the side of the treasure mountain when he remembered a detail that Mila had said about the treasure.

She had said that the city above him used to be a lake before it was drained. That meant that this cavern used to be at least partially submerged in water. Dragons didn't mind water, but he had never heard of one living in the water. Well, not a proper dragon. Leviathans lived in water, but they weren't really dragons, more like an evolutionary cousin to dragons, a bit like monkeys were to humans.

He scooped another handful of coins and gems up, dropping them into the bag. Two or three more scoops would fill the bag.

He tried to remember his schooling. What did a Leviathan do when its water source dried up? He was pretty sure they moved to a new water source; they were able to move and breathe on land, after all.

He scooped up another handful and was about to dump it when he saw one of the coins had been minted, not just cast. He dumped the coins and fished out the stamped one he had spotted.

Looking it over, it was in remarkably good condition. On one side was the imprint of two men facing one another, with writing around the edge he didn't recognize. On the flip side was a shield with what looked like a turkey coming over the top. It looked pretty modern to be in a pile thousands of years old. Finn wasn't sure what had happened after Earth broke down, but he did know there had been a long period when the world descended from modernity.

Then something else Mila had said about this treasure fluttered through his mind.

1520—that was the year she said the gold was dumped in the lake, not thousands of years ago. If there were no dragons left when the gold was dumped, then who had gathered it into a hoard?

Finn swallowed when something caught his attention in the pile. The last scoop of gold had uncovered a sky-blue material. He dropped the coin in the bag and slowly zipped the top closed, not taking his eyes off the patch of sky blue.

The closer he looked, the more he recognized that material. It was bulging upward as if there were an orb under the blue skin, a suspicion that was confirmed when the eyelid opened, revealing a golden-yellow iris with a vertical-slit pupil. The eye blinked once, then swiveled to look directly at him.

The voice of his old teacher echoed in his head. "A leviathan will go into hibernation if its body of water evaporates or is drained. They are patient creatures and know that weather patterns will eventually change, filling their lake once again, even if it takes a thousand years."

The pupil opened wide, changing the mostly golden eyeball to a black deeper than the void.

The mound of coins shifted and began to rain down as the giant head of the coiled Leviathan lifted thirty feet into the air, almost touching the roof of the cavern. The beast began to uncoil, spilling the mound of treasure around it, revealing that the vast bulk of the pile had been the massive snake-like body of the sea serpent.

Finn gulped and discreetly looked at the exit. Ratmen were pouring out of the corridor he had used to enter. Glancing around the cavern, he saw ratmen coming out of the nooks and crannies he had spotted earlier.

"So it was a signal after all," he muttered.

He spied a cave leading out of the cavern, but he

couldn't know if it would eventually lead to the surface. He shrugged; a dwarf was never trapped underground. He would find a way.

He looked up to see the serpent regarding him, and he hoped that maybe it was an actual dragon, with intelligence and reaso—

The leviathan convulsed and breathed ice in a long, powerful spray.

"Nope, just a dumb snake," he yelled, snatching the bag of gold and leaping out of the way of the frost breath.

The bag was heavier than he had expected and slowed him down just enough that the bottom of his boot was hit by the blast, freezing his foot halfway off the floor.

Swinging the bag of treasure like a mace, he smashed it into the ice, shattering the frozen liquid and knocking his foot free. He didn't waste any time and sprinted for the cave while struggling to get the straps of the pack over his shoulders. The hair on his neck tingled, and he dodged to the side as another blast of frost breath left glistening spikes of ice across the ground.

Finn vaulted a cluster of stalagmites, using them for cover from a third blast. Running at full speed, he looked over his shoulder and saw that the ratmen were in hot pursuit, but he welcomed their masses as opposed to the slithering leviathan that they worshiped.

He ducked into the cave just as a blast of cold breath hit the wall and splashed ice across the opening, sealing it shut.

Finn took a second to catch his breath, his hands on his bare knees. He could see the silhouettes of ratmen pounding on the ice, but it was far too thick for them to get through. After a second of consideration, he guessed the leviathan was headed to the tunnel's entrance to clear it for his minions.

"I need to do more cardio," Finn grumbled and started jogging up the cave with nearly a ton of gold on his back, every step reinforced with magic.

It was going to be a long trip home.

CHAPTER TWENTY-ONE

"The first of the townspeople just came around the corner," the curly-haired teenage witch said, poking her head through the cracked door.

Mila nodded, glancing at the rest of the bar. Over the last ten minutes, the three teleporters had transferred the twenty or so townsfolk who had been in the bar and were just now taking the last five.

The elven woman and young Peabrain held hands with the remaining five and formed bubbles as the old man in bibs sat on a chair to catch his breath.

"Harvey, do any of the captured people know how to teleport?" Mila asked.

He thought about it, then nodded. "I think Hester can, and I know Gerry does. I'll pull them aside and let them know what's happening as soon as they get here."

"Thanks." Mila gave him a nod. "Danica, I think you'll have to take a few trips as well. We need to get these people out of here as fast as we can. The longer it takes, the longer we have to fight."

"What if you and Penny need to evacuate during the fight? I don't want to leave you exposed like that," she said with a frown.

"It'll be fine," Mila reassured her with a smile. "If it gets too hairy, Carl and his people can get us out. Besides, I just need you to take the first couple of trips. Once the Rougarou arrive, we'll need you and your bow to pick off targets."

Danica didn't like it, but she nodded. "I get what you're saying, and it makes sense. I just don't want anything to happen to you and Penny. If the two of you died because I wasn't here—" She yelped in surprise as she crushed the mostly empty beer bottle in her prosthetic hand. Her face turned red with embarrassment. "Sorry. Sometimes if I'm not concentrating, it can get away from me."

Mila smiled and went in for a hug, wrapping her arms around the tall woman's waist and squeezing hard. "It's okay. It lets me know how much you care."

Danica laughed and hugged her back. "I don't care about you."

Mila tilted her head back in surprise to look up at the smiling blonde.

"I love you. There's a big difference," she amended.

Mila laughed. "That scared me for a second, asshole. Between you and Penny, I'm surprised I can take anything seriously."

Danica chuckled and kissed her forehead. "People who take things seriously all the time are boring. And they don't live as long."

"Oh? Is that your medical opinion?"

172

"It's a medical fact. I didn't make it up. They've done studies on it," Danica said with a serious face.

Mila narrowed her eyes. "See, that's the stuff I'm talking about. I can't tell if you're serious or not."

"Very serious," Danica said haughtily. "I was so serious that I probably took a good three minutes off my lifespan."

Mila rolled her eyes. "Such an asshole."

The front door opened, and magicals began pouring in. Obviously, the first couple of groups freed had clumped together on the five-mile run from the sawmill. Thankfully, most magicals could call upon magic to increase their endurance, or some of the older people would have burned out during the flight.

Even with the help of their magic, most of the people immediately either found a seat or sat down on the floor, breathing heavily, covered in sweat.

Harvey went to a woman and pulled her to her feet, talking quietly with her before bringing her over to Mila and Danica. "This is Hester. I let her know what we're doing. Can you take her to the condo so she can start transporting people?" he asked Danica.

She reached out to the older woman. "I sure can. Be back in a minute."

She formed a teleportation bubble and vanished as the others teleported back. They looked at all the new people and sighed before gathering the closest to them and preparing to take them.

"Listen up, folks," Mila said, waving a hand for attention. "We are getting you all to a safe place, but we only have so many teleporters, so you'll need to be patient."

There was general mumbling, but it was cut off as more people came into the bar, collapsing from exhaustion.

The two teen witches came rushing in. "The last of them are coming down the street now, but I think the wolfmen are right on their heels. I could hear barking, and it was getting louder," one of them said, clearing the door as it burst open once again.

This time, along with the press of civilians, the G.A.E.L. team, including Nick who was still in bear form, followed them inside. Carl began barking orders.

"We need to hold them off for as long as possible. Tina, start grabbing chairs and tables. I want a barricade across the middle of the room. Howie and Nick, get those three pool tables over here and on their sides. We can reinforce them and use them as the center of the barricade. Jenny, trap the door. Nothing too big, and for the love of God, make it a shaped charge this time."

He clapped his hands. "Come on, people. Clear the area. All civilians to the back of the bar while you wait for transport. Move! We only have a few minutes."

Everyone jumped into action, the civilians scrambling to the back, but a few who were relatively uninjured jumped in and started stacking tables and chairs. Harvey did his concrete trick when the stacks were high enough.

Four men were struggling with one of the pool tables, while Nick in his bear form moved one on his own, and Howard dragged the third across the floor with little effort. In less than a minute, there was a barricade of three pool tables flanked by concrete and furniture walls.

Jenny finished setting up her charges before taking a running leap over the middle pool table. "Clear the door!"

Mila, Penny clinging to her shoulder, crouched beside Carl behind the center table, her Ivar out and Gram extended. "How far behind were they?"

"Only a minute or two," he said, preparing a bubble in one hand.

Mila saw that all the team members had prepared spells and were waiting for a chance to use them. The room had gone quiet after the scrambling rush to get a defense set up.

A popping sound made Mila spin around, her heart in her throat. She relaxed when she saw it was Danica and Hester returning.

Mila pointed the back of the room out to the two confused women. "We moved them back there. Get them out as fast as you can."

Danica nodded, rushing to the back. Her medical training kicking in, she pulled the three worst-injured people she could find together and began forming a bubble.

Howling outside made Mila turn to the door. The sound of popping bubbles behind her told her that more people were getting out. They just needed to hold on for a few minutes.

Another bubble popped, and several people screamed behind Mila just as the front door opened and Jenny's explosive went off.

There were a flash and loud bang, obviously muffled by magical means to not blind and deafen everyone in the bar as the charge went off and blew the door and surrounding wall to splinters, along with the three Rougarou that were scrambling to get in. Their bodies were reduced to fine red mist as the doorway was cleared for a second before a wave of more eight-foot-tall wolfmen poured in.

The G.A.E.L. team opened up with their spells. Carl's bubble shot forward, transforming into a long spear of metal that skewered two Rougarou, the momentum carrying them back to tumble into the street.

Tina's spell hit the dirty old rug and splashed out into a circle, leaving a pink vapor that was almost instantly absorbed by the carpet. After a few seconds, the carpet began to buck and vibrate before exploding into strips several feet long that reached out and wrapped up any legs in the area, pinning several Rougarou in place while they struggled against the restraints.

Tina then pulled her extremely large pistol out and began filling the trapped enemy with large-caliber handgun bullets.

The gun was much quieter than Mila would have suspected until she saw a glowing symbol on the barrel that flashed every time she pulled the trigger. After confirming that the rest of the team had them on their weapons, she assumed it was some sort of silencer spell.

Mila was grateful for the muffled sound in the confines of the bar. Nothing was worse than trying to fight while one of your senses was impaired. She never realized how much she relied on sound in a fight until Finn had made her use noise-canceling headphones for a couple of their sparring sessions.

Penny added her own brand of magical destruction, launching herself at the incoming beasts and flitting from one opponent to another, raking claws at eyes and muzzles, along with sending out searing jets of dragon fire that melted fur and skin alike.

Mila added a bolt of celestial magic from the Ivar to the fight, more out of wanting to contribute than need. The G.A.E.L. team was handling the chokepoint like the true professionals they were.

Mila glanced back to check on how the evacuation was going and nearly collapsed when she saw Seline standing in the middle of the room, her wand out and pointed at the civilians, a mass of dark energy growing on the tip.

Mila didn't think, just reacted. She sprang to her feet, charging in and squeezing off a shot from the pistol as she cocked Gram back for a swing.

Seline seemed to sense her coming and turned in time to put up a spell wall and absorb the celestial bolt before releasing her already prepared spell on the tip of her wand.

Mila had just enough time to turn her arm with the Ivar in it and form a shield, deflecting the blast of black energy upward. It tore a hole in the ceiling, letting in a shaft of dust speckled sunlight.

Mila had not stopped her charge, a trick she had learned from her boyfriend, and swung Gram with everything she had.

Mila felt her magic rush into her arm, giving it more power than she knew she could muster and distracting her slightly as the new ability showed itself. Her swing was not as precise as she would have liked, heading for Seline's chest instead of her neck, but there was still power enough behind the swing to end the witch.

Faster than Mila could track, Seline pulled a dagger from her robes and blocked Gram's path.

The magical dagger showered sparks from the impact. Mila was surprised to see Seline blasted off her feet and into a wooden column. She must have put more power into the hit than she realized.

Mila took the second's reprieve to check on the civilians. She saw Danica pop back into the bar, her eyes going wide at the sight of her fighting with Seline, but she set her jaw and reached out for the next three people and vanished in a blue mist.

Mila blinked, trying to understand what had just happened. It looked like Danica had just teleported without a bubble, but as far as Mila knew, that wasn't possible.

She didn't have time to consider further when movement from the corner of her eye drew her attention back to Seline, who was getting to her feet, her wand flicking forward.

Mila put up her shield, expecting another big spell, but yelped in surprise as a tiny smoking bubble of black and purple magic veered around her shield and slammed into her thigh.

The hit hurt, but it wasn't paralyzing by any means. It did, however, distract Mila enough to let Seline get within striking distance.

The crazed redhead stabbed down with the dagger, hitting Mila's shield and digging the tip of the blade into it. Her wide, insane eyes reflected the golden shine of Mila's shield as it held the point at bay.

Seline hissed a strange word Mila didn't recognize, and black and purple energies flared to life on the bade.

When the tip of the blade energized, it began to send

off gold and black sparks as the opposing energies inter-acted. Slowly the dagger pierced the golden barrier. Seline used her height and size advantage, pushing down with unnatural weight, driving Mila to one knee.

Glancing to the side, Mila saw the last of the civilians vanish in a teleport spell.

"That's it! They're out! A little help over here?" Mila called to anyone who could hear her.

Seline seemed to realize for the first time that there were others in the building with them. She looked around wildly, then pulled back, taking the dagger with her and throwing up a shield of her own.

The move was just in time as dragon fire blasted against the magical barrier, blocking Seline from Mila's sight. Penny flared her wings to hover in front of the shield and keep the fire up.

A second later, Penny's flaming breath passed through the barrier, but Seline was already gone.

Carl slid in next to Mila, wrapping an arm around her and beckoning for Penny to come to him. "Penny, we have to get out of here."

The dragon dove into his outstretched arm and he instantly formed a bubble, teleporting them away.

CHAPTER TWENTY-TWO

M ila blinked against the sudden bright light as they appeared in the center of a group of haggard and scared refugees.

They were on the bottom floor of the condo building she and Finn owned, in one of the two unoccupied units. They hadn't found anyone who needed the unit in the six months it had been ready. The walls were bare, so the only color in the whole place was the honey-brown wood flooring and the golden and pink late evening sunlight coming through the western-facing windows.

Mila stood and was immediately consumed in a hug by Danica. "Fuck, I thought you were in real trouble back there."

Mila hugged her back. "Not going to lie, I thought the same thing."

Penny landed on Mila's shoulder and patted her on the top of the head. "Shir shee."

Mila laughed. "Thanks. I *felt* like a badass."

"Carl is contacting Preston," Howard said, stepping up

behind them, "and letting him know we need to send up a couple more teams to take care of the Rougarou and Seline. I don't suppose you can contact your sisters and let them know about this Azoth character? He sounds like he might be out of our league."

Danica put a hand on her shoulder. "Hey, I'm going to start doing what healing I can. There are still a lot of hurt people here."

Mila pulled her broken sisterhood phone from her pocket and showed it to the orc. "I would love too, but my phone was busted in my first fight with that crazy witch. I don't have another way to contact them until Friday when I don't make my scheduled meeting with them."

He took the phone and inspected it, turning it over in his hands a few times. "This is a pretty nice work of tech and magic." He looked up at her. "I can fix it if you want."

Mila's brows rose. "Really? I didn't know that was possible."

"Sure, anything is possible with enough know-how and magic. Give me a few minutes," he said, turning away and heading for the kitchen counter.

"Shee shir. Chi," Penny called, making the orc turn back.

"I'm sorry Penny I don't speak draconic."

"She asked if she could come watch you perform the repair. She's interested in the process."

He nodded and smiled around his tusks. "It would be a pleasure."

Penny launched herself onto his shoulder, making the huge man start with fright. Mila had to press her lips together hard to keep from laughing. They made their way through the crowded condo, Howard being careful not to push and shove with his huge body.

"Preston sends his thanks," Carl said beside Mila.

She hadn't heard him come over and looked up at him in surprise. "Damn. What is with all you big guys moving around like ninjas?"

"I'm not that big," Carl said, looking down at himself.

"Everyone is big when you're four-ten," Mila said with a smile.

"You tell him, sister," Tina said as she walked past, heading for the front door.

"Did she just speak?" Mila asked, watching the truly tiny witch expertly weave between bodies.

"Height is a sensitive subject for her." He chuckled. "She felt an immediate kinship with you when we met. Wouldn't shut up about it when you weren't around."

"I was just happy there was someone tiny who kicks ass professionally around I could look up to." She cleared her throat. "Metaphorically speaking, of course."

Carl groaned. "I can't believe I didn't think of that one first."

"You joke with your subordinates? Isn't that unprofessional or something?"

He shook his head. "They're not my subordinates. We're professionals, but we don't have a top-down structure. The five of us sit down and decides who's best at what and why. So we know who's in charge and why we all decided to pick them. It just so happens that I'm the best at tactics and quick reasoning, so I'm the de facto leader."

"Interesting," Mila said, trying to find major problems with it.

"It only works on small teams who know each other well. Otherwise, there are trust issues, and that gets messy. We're all friends on and off the job. At this point, I know them better than I do my brothers and sisters."

"How many siblings do you have?" Mila asked, not really knowing what to do until Howard fixed the phone but make small talk.

"Thirteen. Eight brothers and five sisters." He glanced at her and laughed at the open-mouthed stare she was giving him. "My family was very Catholic. No condoms equals lots of babies, plus we were on a farm. My dad always said it was natural to grow crops and livestock, so why not grow your own workforce as well?" He laughed again. "Man, he was a character. He kept complaining that he had to add on to the house every two years because it smelled too much like a barn for people, but he and mom just kept pushing out a new one every year or so."

"That's insane." Mila was gobsmacked.

"What's insane is my youngest sister is twenty-seven, and my parents aren't even sixty yet. My dad just turned fifty-nine, and my mom is only fifty-eight. They were married and having their first kid while my mom was only eighteen." He chuckled. "I can't even imagine having kids that young."

"Speaking of full houses," Mila said, looking around the cramped condo, "what are we going to do with a whole town full of people?"

Most of the people had sat down in small groups, leaning against the walls or lying on the wood floor, still exhausted from the fight and flight. Mila noticed Remmy for the first time, one of the goblins who lived on the second floor, walking among the Elk Riverites with a cloth shopping bag dragging behind her from which she was passing out waters and packages of oyster crackers.

Her green hoodie was up, but her confusingly slim but stocky figure let everyone know she wasn't one of the "normal" races that could walk freely among the Peabrains. She never bothered with concealment spells to hide her greenish skin and sharp features. Instead, she reveled in her goblin-ness and prowess as the top warrior in her tribe, which was evident by her full body tattoo.

Remmy saw her looking her way and gave an over the top wave and smile. Mila smiled and waved back. She liked the little goblin, even if she tended to be naked a lot. Like, *a lot*—in the hallway, in the lobby, when she would come over for some random ingredient while baking, and even once when she just stopped by for a chat. When Mila had asked her why she was always naked, she said, "How else are you supposed to see my tattoos?" then flexed and stuck a power pose. Mila still burst out laughing at the most random times, thinking about that.

Carl brought her back to their conversation. "Preston has temporary housing on the manor grounds. He sent transportation that should be arriving within half an hour to get everyone there."

"He has housing set aside for refugees?"

"You'd be surprised how many times we have to evacuate an area when dealing with a threat. Most evildoers don't care about collateral damage."

"Boy, do I know about that," Mila said, thinking back to all the shit Hermin and Garret had to clean up in her and Finn's wake.

Howard moved through the crowd toward them, extending his arm, the repaired phone in his palm. "Here you are. Good as new."

"Thank you!" Mila turned the phone over in her hands a few times before hitting the power button.

The screen lit up and she entered her code, unlocking the phone.

"Excuse me, gentlemen," she said, heading for the door and stepping out into the lobby.

She quickly pulled up Victoria's number and hit send. The phone rang several times before the sultry voice of Victoria answered.

"Hello?"

"Victoria, it's Mila."

"Yes, I know. I'm on a conference call with the Tokyo office. Can I call you back?" She sounded slightly irritated.

Mila frowned. "No, Victoria. It can't wait." She was pissed. "I know you think of me as a kid, and I can understand that mentality to a degree, but you need to listen to me."

There was a sigh on the other end of the line, which pissed Mila off even more.

"Okay, Mila. What is it you need to say?"

"Heather is dead," Mila started, but Victoria cut her off, obviously wanting to get back to her conference call.

"We already know that, dear. We spoke about it when you dragged me all the way up to Idaho and showed me an empty cave. I said—"

"Will you shut the fuck up and listen to me?" Mila growled, cutting her off.

Victoria cleared her throat. "I'm sorry. Please continue."

"As I was saying, Heather is *dead*, and not as in her body was slain. I mean she is dead for real. Her soul was consumed right from her body. Then her body was turned to dust."

There was silence on the other line for a few beats. When Victoria spoke again, she used a cautious tone. "You must be mistaken. There are very few creatures who could do that to a Valkyrie."

"I know what a soul looks like, Victoria. You watched me cleanse the Dark Star's yourself. It was eaten. I was there, and I saw the whole thing happen, not ten feet away from me."

Now her voice was concerned, the power CEO persona she had been in falling away. "What did this?"

"I spoke with her before she was killed. She told me to tell you that the Drude had returned," Mila said, thinking she got the name right. "Seline referred to him as Lord Azoth."

Mila could hear Victoria swallow hard. "That...that's not possible. I killed him myself," she whispered.

"Evidently, you didn't. Heather said he had gone into a deep slumber, but now he's awakening and consuming the souls of magicals to regain his powers. He's the one who killed her." Mila swallowed a lump in her throat as she remembered the power he possessed and just how close to death she had come. "He's weak, but still too strong for me to fight on my own."

"No!" she shouted, then lowered her voice. "No, do not try to fight that monster. I'll get the sisterhood together and go after him right now. We need to attack while he's still weak."

"Who is he?" Mila asked, her curiosity getting the better of her.

"He was the assassin who followed us when we took passage on *Earth*. He was instructed to steal the Reaper and return it to his master. Many sisters perished during the battle to put him down. He is the antithesis of celestial magic since he is from a race of infernal magic users. Our magics cancel one another out."

"That explains why it was so hard to fight his disciple. She was using some black and purple magic that I had never seen before that ate through my shield like acid."

"Where is Azoth now?" Mila could hear Victoria's heels clacking along as she started running.

"There's a sawmill five miles north of Elk River. That's where they're based, either that or the cave I took you to."

"Okay. I can get the exact location from your phone." Her breathing became more labored as she continued to run. "Good work, little sister. I should have listened to you from the start. Your part is done, now let the sisterhood take care of the rest."

CHAPTER TWENTY-THREE

Mila, Danica, and Penny collapsed onto the big L-shaped couch in their living room, exhausted and hungry.

"You want pizza?" Danica asked, pulling her phone out and turning it on. "I'm ordering pizza."

"Chi," Penny said, a smoke ring floating up from where she had curled into a ball on the back cushion of the couch.

"Agreed. Pizza sounds good," Mila mumbled, looking at the door on the far side of the condo. "If we pay them extra, do you think they'll deliver it to the coffee table? The door is so fucking far away."

"Wow, that is a whole new level of laziness." Danica chuckled, lifting the phone to her ear while it rang.

Unzipping her corset holster, Mila tossed it onto the cushion beside her before unlacing her hiking boots. With great effort, she was finally able to pull them off her feet. Evidently, traipsing through the woods all day and fighting Rougarou was pretty tiring. Who knew?

She dropped the boots beside the couch instead of

putting them away, which really spoke to how tired she was. She couldn't stand to have the house a mess, to the point that she described *herself* as a neat-freak, but she couldn't even muster the motivation to walk the boots to the shoe rack beside the front door.

Her socks got the same treatment, being dropped on top of the boots in two wadded up balls.

Putting her bare feet on the coffee table, she splayed and flexed her toes, reveling in the freedom of move-ment. She felt bad that she was able to relax, knowing that Carl and his team were heading back up there in a few hours when two more teams would be ready to go with them. At least this time, they would be fully prepared.

The transfer of the townsfolk went off without a hitch. The buses arrived within twenty minutes and had everyone loaded up ten minutes later. Harvey had thanked her and Danica profusely for saving his people before being ushered onto the bus by Tina, who had seen how tired they were and taken pity on Mila and Danica, steering the still-talking man away.

Carl had given her his card and said to call him directly if she ever needed fire support in the future. He said he would do his best to get the team there, even if Preston had other plans for them.

Then everyone was gone, and exhaustion caught up with them like a punch to the face. It was all they could do to get to the couch, and now that she was there, Mila had no plans to move until the pizza arrived.

Danica hung up, dropping the phone onto the couch beside her and letting her head flop back. "Thirty to forty minutes. I got three large pizzas. Pineapple on one for you and Penny."

"Thanks," Mila mumbled, falling asleep where she reclined. "Why did you get three?"

"Finn," Danica said, explaining everything.

"You know he won't be back tonight," Mila argued. "There is no way in hell he found Montezuma's gold in one day of searching, and we both know he'll keep looking until he finds it."

"Hey. I made a bet, and I intend to honor it," Danica countered. "My part in that bet is believing he will be home any minute, and we all know he can eat a large pie on his own. He's going to be extra-hungry after hauling all that treasure home."

"Har, har," Mila said, sarcastically. "He's probably having the best tacos of his life in a street-side cafe right now."

Penny raised her head and looked at the door, then started chuckling. Turning to Mila, she smiled.

Mila narrowed her eyes. "What—"

The door burst open, slamming into the doorstop and rebounding closed again.

"Motherfucker!" Finn roared, pushing the door open again and stumbling in.

Mila and Danica both leaped to their feet, eyes wide. Taking in his state, they both stifled laughs. It was so bad that Mila had to clamp her hands over her mouth to not burst into hysterics.

Finn narrowed his eyes and stared them both down. "What's so funny?"

Tears were running down Mila's cheeks as she held it

in. She pointed at his shirt. "Are...are you wearing a crop top?"

Danica couldn't take it and burst into wailing laughter, pointing at his pants, or what was left of them. "And Daisy Dukes?"

Finn frowned and looked down at himself, then turned to the floor-to-ceiling mirror behind the small bench they stored shoes under and looked at himself for what was obvious to Mila was the first time since he had left the condo that morning.

His frown turned into a grudging smile. "I suppose I am."

That was all it took for Mila to lose it. She fell onto the couch in uncontrollable laughter.

Even Penny was laughing, sending spouts of fire into the air.

Finn lost his smile as the laughter went on for quite a bit longer than he thought necessary.

He loudly proclaimed over the laughs, "I'm going to take a shower. I have this here bag of treasure that I'm going to put beside my door. It would be a shame if a dragon were to steal it for their hoard." He then grumbled something, but Mila couldn't hear what it was.

He stalked down the hall toward them, the frown on his face making his dirty beard puff out. The sight sent Mila into another round of laughter, but when he got close, she sucked in a breath and nearly vomited from the smell.

"Oh, my God." She swallowed the rising lump in her throat. "Is that shit all over your legs?"

Danica suddenly stopped laughing and started gagging.

"Raw sewage, actually, so probably more than just shit."

Finn smiled sadistically as he stopped beside the couch and let them take in the stench.

"For the love of God, babe! Please go get in the shower. I'll bring a trash bag to throw those things into," Mila begged, backing away from him.

He chuckled. "Good call. I don't think I can pull this look off anyway."

Mila saw the backpack for the first time. "No. Fucking. Way. You found it?"

He stopped and looked over his shoulder. "I told you it would be easy." He gave her a brilliant smile and continued across the mats, his boots leaving what Mila decided she would think of as muddy prints.

Carefully slipping one arm out of the backpack, Finn gently lowered it to the floor. Even though he was being careful, the room still shook when he let go of the bag. There was an audible groan of wood as the obviously heavy bag settled. Satisfied the bag was not going to fall over, he opened the door to their room and went in, closing it behind him.

Mila looked at Danica with wide eyes. "I can't believe he actually did it."

"Looks like someone owes Finn a ride on Death Machine," Danica said, winking and giving Mila finger guns.

"Why did he have to name his motorcycle 'Death Machine?'" she muttered.

"Because he's hilarious. Especially when he doesn't mean to be."

Mila snorted. "That's true." She looked at the "mud" stains. And sighed. Not putting shoes away she could do, but leaving that mess to dry was out of the question. "I'll go get the mop."

"You might want to get some bleach too," Danica suggested with a frown.

"Oh, yeah. For sure, going to use some bleach on that."

CHAPTER TWENTY-FOUR

After cleaning up the mess Finn had inadvertently tracked through the house, Mila went and got a plastic trash bag from under the sink and headed for her and Finn's room.

Danica stepped out of her room and nearly ran into Mila.

"Oh, hey. I just got off the phone with Phil," Danica said, leaning on her doorframe. "We're heading over to the Refinery for some drinks and karaoke later tonight. You and Finn want to come?"

"Uh, I'm pretty tired. When are you thinking of going?"

"Yeah, I'm pretty tired too, but I haven't seen him in a few days. I said I needed to shower and take a nap first, so we're meeting at ten."

Mila pulled her phone out and checked the time—6:52 pm. "Holy hell. How is it only seven? I feel like we've been up for days."

Danica smiled. "What can I say? We can take out supervillains and be home by dinner. We're just that good."

Mila laughed and hugged her friend. "I love you. You're such an idiot. How can I say no to karaoke with you?"

"I'm guessing you can't?" she said hopefully.

"We're in. But," Mila held up a finger and raised her brows in mock seriousness, "we have to sing *We are the Champions*."

Danica snorted a laugh. "Now who's the idiot? Of course we were going to sing that. At this point, it's *our* song. Duh."

"Okay, get in there and get a shower. Don't want to see Phil smelling like wet dog, do you?" Mila said, skipping away.

She stuck her tongue out at Danica from over her shoulder, but it turned to a scream when she saw that Danica had rushed up on her. The elf slapped her ass, sending a shock up Mila's spine.

"That's rich, coming from someone who smells like wet dog *and* raw sewage." Danica pinched her nose and waved away the stink while making a sour face.

"Okay, okay. I see how it is," Mila said in a cocky voice as she backed away, a hand rubbing her sore ass. "You better watch your back, Meadows. I gotta revenge slap locked and loaded."

Danica crossed her arms and stuck her nose in the air. "Please. I have an ass made of rock. You would break your little hand on it before I felt a thing."

Mila backed to the corner and turned to cross the dojo, keeping narrowed eyes on Danica the whole time. Just before she backed all the way around the corner, she held two fingers in a V, pointing at her eyes, then at Danica.

"I know where you sleep, Meadows."

Danica laughed before disappearing into her room. "You really do need a shower, by the way. I wasn't joking," she called from her room.

Mila sniffed her armpit and had to agree.

She saw Penny, her hands clasped behind her back and a worried look on her face, inspecting the backpack sitting between their room's doors.

"What's wrong?" Mila asked, squatting beside the obviously troubled dragon.

Penny stopped pacing and stared at the bag. "Shir. Chi chi, shee."

Mila's brows rose. "I don't think it was too much to ask. Finn was eager to help you, and you know how much he likes doing this kind of stuff."

Penny nodded and smacked the side of the full backpack, making a clinking sound. "Chi shee?"

"I don't know, a couple hundred pounds?" Mila guessed.

"Squee."

Mila frowned, looking from Penny to the pack. "That can't be right. How the fuck is he supposed to be able to carry an actual ton of gold? That's ridiculous."

Penny explained and Mila listened, fascinated by the hidden abilities of dwarves. Then Penny explained the problem, and Mila understood her concerns.

Mila reached out and took the small dragon's hand, giving it a squeeze. "I'll talk to him about it. Don't worry, between the two of us, we can keep him in line."

Penny pursed her lips and raised an eye ridge at the comment, making Mila snort a laugh.

"Okay, maybe 'in line' is a bit much, but I bet we can make him see reason. He's a smart guy."

Penny waggled a hand at chest level and shrugged.

"Now you're just being mean." Mila laughed, standing and unfolding the trash bag. "Okay, I need to get those clothes into the garbage as soon as possible. I just hope he didn't throw them on the floor." She looked down at the pack. "You want help 'stealing' that into your room?"

Penny shook her head and pointed at her own chest. "Shir chi."

Mila shook her head in wonder. "Someday, you and I are going to sit down, and you're going to explain faerie dragon culture to me. It's fascinating."

Penny nodded, then shooed her to her room. "Chi."

"You're welcome," Mila said before closing the door.

To her great relief, there was not a pile of shit-stained clothes on the floor of their bedroom. She was also surprised to see that there were no footprints on the hardwood. In fact, she couldn't smell it.

The shower was running, and she could hear Finn singing an awful off-key melody. She had to give him credit for singing at the top of his lungs, though. She stepped into the white-tiled bathroom and leaned on the doorframe, crossing her arms, and just took it all in for a minute.

The one thing Finn had insisted on when they expanded the condo was that the bathrooms be amazing, and their contractor Kevin hadn't disappointed.

The room was twice as big as a lot of the bedrooms Mila had had growing up. A huge slab of black granite made up the long double-sink counter on the left, with a mirror that covered the entire wall from the counter to the ceiling. To the right was a smaller room with a door that held the toilet bidet combo along with its own sink. Next to that was their walk-in closet with room for hanging clothes and built-in drawers and shelves for a hundred pairs of shoes that wasn't even an eighth of the way full. A nice big white leather ottoman had been set in the center of the closet to sit on while dressing.

In the very center of the bathroom was a tub made of formed black granite that matched the counters but had been made from a single piece of rock. Finn had used his dwarven earth magic to form the perfectly-shaped tub that somehow was as hard as stone but unbelievably comfortable to sit in.

But Mila was looking at the back wall of the room where clear glass-enclosed a black stone floor-to-ceiling shower with about twenty shower heads, all controlled from a digital touchscreen built into the wall.

She didn't want to know how much Finn had spent on the room, but Kevin had said in passing that he had built entire houses for less.

Their bathroom was by far the nicest room in the whole building. Hell, it was probably the nicest room in a three-block radius.

Caterwauling while scrubbing himself clean with a loofah on a stick, Finn stood in the shower with his back to the door. She looked him over, amazed that history had gotten dwarves so wrong.

Finn sang with gusto, if not talent. *"It's sooo typical of me to talk about myself, I'm sooooorrrrryyy."*

Six-five and nearly three feet wide at the shoulders, Finn was a huge and imposing figure. His artificial arm somehow added to his attractiveness, as if the woven yellow diamond were a natural extension of his body, both odd and beautiful at the same time.

She watched the muscles of his back flexing as he scrubbed his prosthetic, plunging the loofah between the open diamond weave, making sure nothing hid in the nooks and crannies.

"I hope that you're wellll. Did you ever make it out of that town where nothing ever haaaaaappened?"

The dirty clothes were nowhere to be seen, and she feared he had thrown them in the hamper, but when she stepped into the bathroom proper, she saw them piled in the tub. She smiled when she realized that he had not only washed them, but he must have used a rag to clean the floor after taking his boots off.

She opened the trash bag and stuffed the wrung-out but still quite damp remains of clothes into it, including the rag. She almost threw the boots in for good measure, but finding boots in his size was a problem. He *had* cleaned them thoroughly, so she left them in the tub to dry and tied off the bag, sealing the offending clothes in, and dropped it by the door before heading into her closet to get undressed.

"It's no secret that the both of us are running out of time."

She was still trying to figure out what the hell he was singing. It was so bad it was almost art all on its own, like when someone tapes a banana to a wall and calls it expressionism. The melody was vaguely familiar, at least what she could pick out, but his timing was as bad as his tone, making the whole thing a staccato jumble of words.

She opened the hamper and dropped her sweater and socks in, then stripped her leggings off and tossed them in after. Removing her bra, she hung it on a hook beside the built-in dresser and mirror combo. Then tossed her underwear in the dirty clothes and closed the lid.

She leaned into the mirror, looking herself in the eye before her gaze wandered across her face, looking for anything out of place with her skin. As usual these days, she didn't find anything, leaving her with a strange disappointment.

Ever since her magic had come to life in earnest, she'd noticed that her skin was clearer than it had ever been, along with her hair and nails becoming oddly strong and shiny. She knew it was due to having more magic in her system all the time, but her scientific mind wanted to know *why* the magic made her skin clearer.

As she walked out of the closet and toward the shower, she watched in confused horror as Finn held the loofah like a microphone, singing into the fluffy ball on the end of the stick. He had his eyes closed and really belted out the chorus.

"So hello from the other siiiiiiide!"

Mila's eyes went wide as she finally realized what he was singing.

"I must have called a thousand tiiiiiiimes!"

His butt clenched when he hit the high note and she choked out a laugh, her hand going to her mouth to hide the smile she was afraid might split her face in two.

Finn's eyes popped open and he spun around, the loofah on a stick still held in front of his face.

"Oh, my God. Were you just singing Adele?"

He stood up straight, putting his hands on his hips. "I'll have you know she's a national treasure."

Mila walked around to the side of the glass and stepped into the huge shower with him. She walked up and put a hand on his chest, gently pushing him back until she was in the streams as well.

Her face hurt, she was smiling so much. "You know she's from England, right? Don't you need to be *from* a country to be a national treasure *of* that country?"

He gave her a disapproving look, the water running through his hair and down his nose. "Not if you're as badass as Adele."

Mila laughed, then put her arms around his neck and pressed herself against him. She let the water flow over them, the liquid warming her as much as he was.

"Hi," she whispered, looking up at him. "I missed you today."

He smiled, his wet beard parting enough that she could see his white teeth. "I missed you too."

She felt his hand rest on the small of her back, holding her close as he gazed into her eyes. He began to sway ever so slowly as if he were leading her in a dance to music only he could hear. They stayed like that for three long breaths, just enjoying each other's closeness.

"Are we dancing to Adele?" she asked when his movements became more pronounced.

He stopped the swaying, the barest hint of amused guilt in his eyes. "National treasure, darlin'."

She chuckled, pressing her cheek to his chest, letting the warm water run through her hair.

Then the loofah was slowly inserted into her armpit, and he twisted it back and forth to soap her up.

She barked a laugh. "Thanks. Am I that stinky?"

"There is the distinct smell of wet dog on you," he said, starting to scrub her in earnest. "What the hell did you get up to today? Were you at a dog park?"

She let go of his neck and stepped back to run her hands through her hair, wetting it down and removing any large debris she found while Finn continued to scrub her.

He handed her the bottle of shampoo, then pumped more soap onto the loofah.

She squirted some of the vanilla-scented shampoo into her hand and gave the bottle back to Finn. Turning her back to him, she stepped out of the shower stream and began to massage it in.

Finn used the opportunity to really get after some grime just above her lower back tattoo.

"Truthfully, we had a pretty intense day," Mila said, pulling her long hair over her shoulder and washing the ends while Finn worked.

He started chuckling, making Mila frown and look over her shoulder at him. He was staring at her tattoo and shaking with laughter. He saw her looking and clamped his lips shut.

"What?" she asked, suspecting she knew what he was laughing at. It was her personal mark of shame, an impulse decision during undergrad. She hated that she still had it, but she never seemed to have the time to remove it. Then again, most of the time, she forgot it was there.

"I'm sorry, darlin'." He cleared his throat and continued in a much steadier voice, "I just don't understand why you still have this tattoo. A cartoon little boy and a tiger? I mean, it's just so ridiculous, and not you at all."

She sighed. "It was a popular comic when I was in

college. We all went to get tattoos, but I didn't have any idea what I wanted, so I said the first thing that came to mind." Her shoulders sagged. "There might have been alcohol involved."

"Then why not remove it, or change it to something you want?" He pulled her back into the stream of warm water, and hanging the loofah on a hook, began to rinse her hair for her.

"Because I don't ever have the time to go to all those laser treatments. It's a pain in the ass to remove a tattoo."

He laughed. "No, it's not. I can do it right now if you want. Or I can rearrange the ink into something else."

"How can you remove a tattoo?" She dropped her chin to her chest in defeat before nodding. "Magic."

Finn nodded along. "Yeah. Magic."

Mila lifted her head and sucked in a deep breath. "You know what, it's dealer's choice on this one. You're the only one who sees it regularly, so you decide what to do with it. I'm going to be over here conditioning my hair. Don't mind me."

He handed her the conditioner. "Are you sure? It's your body. I don't want to do something you don't like."

Mila shrugged. "Babe, I trust you more than anyone on the planet. You can do whatever you want to my body," she said, coyly looking over her shoulder as she handed the conditioner back.

He took the bottle and smiled. "I have an idea."

"Is it about the tattoo?" she asked, massaging the conditioner into her scalp.

"Yeah."

"Well, that's disappointing," she joked.

"Oh, don't worry. I have those ideas too. They're for later."

Mila gasped in an over-the-top manner. "Such a tease."

"Will you hold still? This takes precision," he said, grabbing her hip with one hand.

She smiled, reached down, and put her hand over his, sliding her slender fingers between his. He gave her fingers a light squeeze with his thick digits.

"Babe, just one thing before you begin."

"What?"

She swallowed, looking him in the eye over her shoulder. "Don't give me an Adele-themed tramp stamp."

He snorted a laugh and rolled his eyes. "You're hilarious."

CHAPTER TWENTY-FIVE

"What does it mean?" Mila asked, her back facing the mirror as she looked over her shoulder at her new tattoo.

It was a black circle with a vertical line through the middle, then what looked like two Vs, their points overlaying the center line equidistant apart, with the points of the Vs facing down.

Finn was watching her as he reclined on the bed they had just spent the last hour "napping" in. "It's the dwarven rune for 'shield maiden.'"

"Come on, babe. Get dressed. We need to meet Danica and Phil in an hour. If you want to take a ride on the bike first, we need to get moving."

"We could always take a ride, then come back here," Finn said, waggling his eyebrows at her.

She just rolled her eyes and turned back to the mirror.

He finally relented and stood, then headed for the closet.

As he passed Mila, she smacked his ass. "Hey. Good

work there. I'm leaving you a five-star review." She gave him a thumbs-up.

He chuckled. "I love how weird you are. Have I ever told you that?"

"Once or twice."

"Did I do that to you?" he asked, suddenly concerned and leaning down to inspect her thigh.

She looked down and saw a dark spot on her thigh. It looked like a bruise and was a little tender to the touch. She tried to remember when she had hit her leg on something, but nothing came to mind. "No, it wasn't you. I probably just walked into something today. It happens."

He leaned in and gave the bruise a kiss, then headed to the closet.

Mila looked at the bruise again, and it came to her. That was the spot Seline's spell had hit her in their last fight. It must have only been a distraction, but she guessed it could have easily left a bruise.

"Where would you even leave the review for that?" he asked after going into the closet and a few seconds later coming back out with jeans while pulling a black t-shirt over his head.

"Oh, there are places, buddy. Trust me," Mila said, taking one last look at the tattoo and deciding she loved it. It was a hell of a lot better than what she'd had before. "Shield maidens, like the ones from Norse mythology?"

"Probably?" Finn shouted from out of sight. "In dwarven culture, there's a story of women who were so fierce in battle that they became the personal guard of the first dwarven king. They were the best of the best, quick and deadly, but more than anything, they were smart. They didn't win their battles because they were stronger, but because they out-thought the enemy. To be called a shield maiden by a dwarf is high praise, and not done lightly."

She walked into the closet, opened her underwear drawer, selected a pair of black cheekies and stepping into them, and asked, "If it's such a special title, should I have it tattooed on me? I don't want to be disrespectful."

Finn sat on the ottoman and pulled on a sock before resting his elbow on his knee and glancing at her as she worked the underwear into the right position. "Yeah. It's absolutely appropriate for you to have it tattooed on you. That's what they do to mark themselves as different from others."

Mila chuckled. "I get that." She pulled a camisole off its hanger and slipped it over her head. "What I mean is, I'm not a shield maiden, so maybe I shouldn't have it tattooed on me."

Finn pulled his other sock on. "Who do you think selects the warriors to become shield maidens?"

"The king?" Mila guessed, selecting a pair of gray leggings and stepping into them. Then, remembering they were going to be riding on the motorcycle, she opted for something a little more substantial.

"Yup. The king. That's me, and I select you. You are my shield maiden," he said, bowing with a flourish.

"You're not a king, though. You're a prince, but isn't your father still the king?" She folded the leggings and put them back in the drawer, then pulled out a pair of low-rise jeans. Stepping into them, she had to jump and pull to get the stiff material over her ass.

"He's the king of all that stuff out there. I'm the only

dwarf on Earth, so on this one planet, I'm the dwarf king," he said, tying his boot.

Mila put on a gray V-neck t-shirt and grabbed a red hoodie from its hanger. "Well then, I think it's official." She curtsied to him. "My lord. Shall we take your steed out and put it through its paces?"

"God, you are really bad at curtsying," he said in mock horror.

"Some girls are graceful, and some girls are me," Mila said with a smile. She pulled on a pair of calf-high black leather boots without a heel. "Ready."

"Me too."

They headed out into the living room and found Penny watching a reality TV show. Mila noticed the treasure bag was empty and was impressed that she had been able to move it all in an hour and a half.

"Hey, Penny. We're going for a ride on the bike—"

"Death Machine," Finn interrupted.

Mila rolled her eyes. "A ride on Death Machine before we head to the bar. You want to come with?"

Penny looked at the TV, and seeing two women in tights in the middle of an obviously staged cat-fight, nodded. "Chi."

"Where's Danica?" Mila asked, seeing that her door was open and the room was empty.

"Shir shee." She held up a note in Danica's handwriting.

Mila took it and read it quickly. "Oh, fuck. Now I feel bad. Sorry we didn't join you guys."

Penny shrugged and made a ring with her finger and thumb, then inserted the finger of her other hand into the ring.

"Gross," Mila said, giving her a narrow-eyed stare before smiling. "But also true."

"What happened?" Finn asked from the coatrack.

"I forgot that we ordered pizza. They ate without us." Mila finished the note and put it in her hoodie pocket. "It also looks like Danica headed to the bar early. She'll meet us there."

"Sounds good. Hey, you never did tell me what you ended up doing today," Finn said, pulling on a worn leather motorcycle jacket he had found in a thrift store that miraculously fit him.

"Oh, man. I think you're going to like this one. Penny can remind me of any details I miss," Mila said, leading the way out the door.

"Did you guys have fun?"

"More or less."

Mila held on tight as Finn gave Death Machine more gas and leaned into the sweeping turn.

They had gotten out of the city and into the mountains without any problems, and Mila had to admit that riding with Finn was a much better experience than riding with Danica. For starters, Finn was a much more solid person to cling to, and he turned out to be a very conscientious driver. But the biggest difference was that the Triumph Bonneville, the bike the tricked-out Death Machine was built from, was a much more stable motorcycle than the piece-of-shit dirt bike Harvey had lent them.

It also helped that they had helmets with radios in

them, so they could talk without shouting. Penny, who was riding in Mila's hood, was out of luck on the conversation front, but she didn't seem to mind in the least. Mila could feel her little body curled into a ball in the hood on her back, and every once in a while, there was a muffled shout of joy from her when Finn took a turn at high speed.

Mila had to admit she was starting to enjoy herself.

"So, you fought Rougarou and a crazy witch who was trying to raise a fucking Drude from its slumber, and you waited this long to tell me about it?"

"Well, I knew it would come up eventually," Mila said.

"That would have been the first thing I said when I got home if it happened to me. Sounds like you had all the fun."

Mila laughed. "Only you would think what I just told you was fun."

Finn chuckled, then focused on the winding mountain road.

The bruised spot on Mila's leg started to ache and she reached down to rub at it through her jeans, but it only seemed to get worse. The ache started to burn. At first, it was just a mild warmness, but after a few minutes, it felt like she had rubbed hot pepper oil into the skin in that one spot.

"Hey, pull over. I think there's something wrong with my leg," Mila said, putting pressure on the spot with the palm of her hand.

"Uh, there's not much room on this road. I think there's a pull-off about a mile up. Would that be okay?"

"Yeah, I think I can tough it out, but don't be afraid to go a little faster," she encouraged.

Finn took the hint and fed the bike more gas.

They were all alone out on the seldom-used road, the only light was from the still-rising moon and the bike's headlight. So when they made a fairly sharp blind turn, Finn never saw the four eight-foot-tall Rougarou waiting for them in the middle of the road.

Finn jammed the handlebars to the side while slamming on the brakes. The bike slid out from under them, and Mila could feel them going down.

Instinctively she threw up a shield, but instead of the normal half-sphere shape, she created a complete sphere around her, Finn, and Penny.

Golden light flashed all around them as the shield hit the ground and rolled, sending them tumbling but protecting them from damage.

Finn managed to wrap Mila in his arms and keep them from flailing into one another.

Eventually, the sphere shield rolled them into the mountain and they came to a crashing stop.

After they had fully stopped, Finn loosened his grip on her. "You okay?"

She nodded. "Penny?"

The dragon crawled out of her hood and gave them a thumbs-up.

Mila pulled her helmet off and took a look around. Her breath caught in her throat when she saw a dozen Rougarou on the road, stalking toward them.

"I'm guessing your work followed you home," Finn said, pointing the other way on the road.

Mila saw a figure in a long dark coat and red pigtails come out of the darkness, a maniacal grin on her face.

"This isn't good, Finn. We can't handle this on our

own." Mila reached for her phone to call Victoria and felt a chill run up her spine. She checked her pockets to be sure, but she remembered leaving the phone on the bedside table.

"Finn?" Mila said slowly, watching Seline stalking toward them and knowing that Azoth could be out there just waiting to consume them.

"Yeah?"

"I don't have my phone. I can't call Victoria to come and help."

Finn pursed his lips, looking from the Rougarou to Seline on the other side. "You think you can take the witch?"

Mila's eyes went wide. She was about to say no, but then she remembered the tattoo Finn had created for her, and she felt ashamed that she would give up so easily. A true shield maiden would fight with tooth and nail if need be. She would do the same.

"Yeah. I can take the bitch," Mila growled, reaching back for her Ivar and Gram, and realizing she didn't have her corset harness on. "There might be a little problem, though."

Finn pulled out Fragar's handle and activated it with a whispered word. The short hook-bladed axe unfolded and glowed purple with dwarven power. Its surface was covered in so many runes that there was barely an unmarked surface on the entire weapon.

He handed the axe to Mila. "I noticed you forgot your weapons. Should probably make a habit of always having them. You know, for next time."

Mila took Fragar and swallowed. She had used the axe

before in practice, but this was the first time she would use it in battle. She felt like she should apologize to the weapon.

"Penny, I need you to fly back to the condo and send a message to Victoria. Azoth has followed me to Denver, and they need to get here as fast as possible. How fast can you get home?"

Penny glanced toward the city and did a quick bit of math. "Shir."

"Okay, we can hold out for five minutes," Mila said, her confidence coming back a little. "I hope."

Finn took her face in his hands. "You are a mother-fucking Valkyrie. You pulled the soul from the Dark Star. You've cut down your enemies to make a path of blood to victory more times than I can count. This is no different. That's why you're my shield maiden—because you're unstoppable. You deserve to win. You have to win so that others might live. That woman is evil, and we vanquish evil. This is your fight."

Mila felt her hackles rise in anticipation at his words. He was right; she was more than capable of doing this. She had to win. There wasn't any other choice.

"Right," she said, her brow furrowed in concentration as she stared Seline down. "Let's do this."

CHAPTER TWENTY-SIX

"Hello?" Seline's childlike voice cut through the growling Rougarou. "You in the shield. Miss Valkyrie. Can you come out? My Lord wants to eat you."

"Wow." Finn shook his head in bewilderment. "You did not exaggerate how creepy that is."

"Did you like my little trick?" Seline smiled. "I knew you were going to get away, so I put a tracking spell on you. And as a bonus, I can make it hurt!"

She pulled out her wand and traced a pattern in the air, and searing pain exploded in Mila's leg.

Mila screamed at the shock but quickly clamped her jaw shut, willing herself to fight through it. She could endure. She was stronger than this psycho. She was a Valkyrie.

Heat was building in the back of her skull, but unlike the searing pain in her leg, this heat was the warm pool of magic that resided in her, golden and pure. It wanted to be set free. It *needed* to be set free.

The first thing Victoria had taught Mila was how

Valkyrie magic worked. It was unique in the universe because, unlike all other magic that worked by the caster's desire, a Valkyrie's magic worked by their conviction.

Mila hadn't really understood what Victoria was saying until now. She wasn't even sure Victoria truly understood the concept. But somehow, Finn understood. He hadn't given her that pep talk to rile her up, he was giving her the keys to her conviction.

No one should live in fear of a tyrant.

This witch was a tyrant. Her Lord was a tyrant. In order to stop them, her powers would obey to the best of their ability.

And just like that, the warm pool of magic trapped at the back of her skull was set free.

She felt warmth spread through her, scrubbing her clean all impurities and filling her with a newfound strength. When the magic reached Seline's tracking spell, it obliterated it, removing the infernal magic from existence.

Mila noticed her vision was sharper and cut through the darkness with ease. Her hearing more acute, letting her not only hear more but process it as well.

She felt like she had woken up for the first time in her life.

"Finn." Mila smiled, focusing on Seline, who was shaking her wand, not understanding why Mila wasn't crying out in pain.

"Yeah, darlin'?" he rumbled.

"You are the best thing that's ever happened to me. You just unlocked a puzzle that's been driving me nuts for six months."

"Glad I could help. You'll have to tell me what I did

later," he said with a smile as he eyed the swaying pack of Rougarou.

Mila laughed. "I love you so much. I just want to bite your toes off."

"What the fuck?"

She laughed. "It's called 'cute aggression.' Look it up when we get home. It's very common."

"I'll trust you on this one. I don't think I want to look up "biting toes" on the Internet."

"Shee?" Penny interrupted.

"Right. Sorry. On three," Mila said, hefting Fragar with one hand and setting her legs for a quick start.

"One." Seline seemed to finally understand that her tracking spell was gone.

"Two." The number of wolfmen had grown to over thirty.

"Three," Mila whispered the power word for her mythril armor.

The shield dropped, and Penny shot into the air faster than Mila had ever seen the dragon move.

Mila heard and felt Finn roar behind her as he charged the pack of Rougarou, meeting his battle cry with howls. With her newly enhanced hearing, Mila heard the distinct sound of Finn ripping the arm off a Rougarou and start using it as a weapon.

Saline pointed her wand at Mila and shot a smoking infernal orb directly at her face.

Using her newly magic-infused body, Mila didn't even attempt to use her shield to block the orb instead side-stepping it completely and charging in close, Fragar held low and behind her.

Seline's eyes went wide, and she smiled in delight. "So fast!" She giggled, pulling her dagger from the folds of her coat.

Mila swung Fragar in an uppercut when she was within striking distance, the axe whistling as it sought its target. Seline's dagger was up in time to deflect the heavy axe, forcing Mila to spin away with Fragar's momentum. Mila added power to the spin and brought Fragar around in a chop aimed at Seline's stomach.

The witch had hopped out of reach and was aiming a wand in Mila's direction, black smoke roiling off the tip.

Mila crouched and powered her shield just in time as deep violet lightning shot from the wand and struck the golden shield with several thick continuous bolts. Mila watched as the two-inch-thick lightning bolt crawled across the shield, sending up trails of golden sparks and casting the road in an eerie flickering purple light.

Spreading out her senses, Mila found a large red harvester ant colony a few yards off the road, spreading throughout the cliff face. Before today she had to speak with an insect to have any kind of effect on it, but with her magic now open to her, she found that she could communicate with a thought.

She sent the colony a mental image of Seline, along with a strong impression that she was a danger to the colony. The response was instant.

Thousands of red harvester ants boiled up from the numerous entrances to the colony and converged on Seline.

Mila was holding the lightning at bay, but she could feel the drain on her power reserves. It needed to stop soon, or she wouldn't have anything left in the tank. She urged the ants to move faster, but the tiny insects were already coming as fast as they could.

Ten seconds later, the first ants were climbing up Seline's boots and into the cuffs of her dark jeans. Another ten seconds, and there were thousands of the tiny creatures spreading throughout her clothes.

Mila couldn't wait any longer and sent the mental command to bite. The ants chomped down with powerful bites, while at the same time slamming their stingers into Seline's soft flesh.

To Mila's relief, the lightning stopped almost instantly as Seline threw her head back and gave a throat-rending screech of pain that made Mila cringe. Several of the Rougarou yelped in pain as their sensitive ears were hit doubly hard from the sonic attack.

Not wasting the opportunity, Mila dropped her shield and charged, Fragar raised above her head prepared for a two-handed strike.

When Seline burst into black and red flames, Mila considered that maybe thousands of ants were overkill. The heat from the infernal flames made Mila jump back or be burned. Backpedaling ten feet, Mila still felt the intense heat tightening the skin on her face. The scream died, along with the flames, revealing a naked Seline, her clothes incinerated by the intense heat. All that remained was her wand.

The redheaded woman was pale and gaunt, her ribs visible through her paper-thin skin, along with spidery blue veins. There were thousands of red bumps across her body, each marking where an ant had delivered its painful dose of venom. Her face was a mask of rage and hate.

"That wasn't very nice," she said in a singsong voice as she crouched and retrieved a second wand that must have been in her coat pocket.

Mila narrowed her eyes and charged in, Fragar held to the side and leaving one hand free.

Seline did exactly what Mila thought she would. The first wand shot out an infernal orb, which Mila batted away with her shield and followed with Fragar swinging in. The second wand shot an orb as well at Mila's seemingly exposed stomach.

Expecting the second shot, Mila pulled the axe close, formed a second shield over that arm, and kept charging at full speed.

The second orb exploded on to the shield half a second before Mila slammed it into Seline's chest and face, smearing the flaming black liquid back onto its creator— not that it would do much damage, but it would stick to her and hopefully blind her for a few seconds.

The impact made Seline stumble back several steps, but unfortunately, none of the burning liquid stuck to her face, though there were several patches on her chest and arm.

She retaliated with more infernal lightning, forcing Mila to take cover behind her already overtaxed shield. Then the second wand laid into the shield as well, and Mila felt her powers beginning to wane. As she watched, several patches of shield thinned. Mila had to dump more power into it, eating even more of her still-fledgling powers.

"Just give up!" Seline shouted in frustration, doubling

her efforts and enlarging the diameter of each bolt by half an inch.

Mila gasped in pain as her magic was sucked into mitigating the enhanced abuse. She gritted her teeth. "Never."

Seline let out a teeth-clenched scream. "Fine. If you won't go down, then maybe your big stupid boy toy will."

The lightning striking the shield halved as Seline aimed her second wand at Finn's exposed back while he fought three Rougarou at once.

Mila needed to think. She couldn't defeat this woman with raw power; Seline was just too powerful. She needed to outthink her. Needed to get in close enough to use Fragar without her being able to block the attack, but she was always on guard.

Mila's eyes widened as she figured out what to do.

The second wand grew a black and purple infernal orb on the end, smoke rising from it like a lit rocket. As soon as Mila saw the orb begin to move, she detached her shield, left the cover of the quickly crumbling construct behind, and dove into the path of the orb.

The infernal missile struck her in the lower ribs, exploding with the force of a sledgehammer and knocking her to the ground, where she rolled several times. A loud crunch of bone snapping accompanied by a cry of pain was the last thing Mila heard before rolling to a stop.

Mila ended up face-down, her right arm caught under her torso and the left broken, bent and twisted at an odd angle below the elbow.

Seline approached cautiously, but when she saw the broken arm, she squatted and poked it hard. There was no reaction from Mila, so she did it again, harder this time. There was still no reaction.

A long-drawn-out roar, followed by the yelping of a Rougarou, then what sounded like a melon being smashed on the pavement drew Seline's attention. She saw the large man standing over three dead wolfmen; the last one had had its head smashed in when the big man stomped on it.

Seline began to excitedly clap at the gory scene, looking down to see if Mila had seen it too, but remembered that she had knocked the Valkyrie out.

Mila's eyes popped open and she rolled over faster than Selina knew was possible, her good arm flashing out in an arc. Seline jumped back.

When she went to land, Seline had an odd sensation of falling too far before she hit the ground on her back. She tried to spring to her feet, but it didn't work. She attempted the slower method of simply standing up, but that didn't work either. She just couldn't get her legs under her to get the proper leverage.

Not understanding, she lifted her legs and blinked a few times, trying to comprehend the bloody stumps that looked like her thighs, but from which the knees, shins, and feet were missing. She looked past her bloody stumps and saw the rest of her legs lying on the ground in front of a very conscious Mila, who was holding a blood-covered axe.

Seline began to scream.

CHAPTER TWENTY-SEVEN

Mila looked down as her severely broken arm with a clinical eye, assessing just how bad it was. There was no pain, but she knew that wasn't going to last much longer as her magical reserves slowly drained.

She had somehow magically disconnected her mind from the pain, knowing it was the only way to pretend to be unconscious to draw Seline in close enough to take out.

It looked like both the radius and ulna had snapped. She carefully slipped the broken appendage into the pass-through pocket of her hoodie, using it as a makeshift sling. It was better than having it flop around.

Seline started screaming, shaking Mila back to the present. She shook her head and felt a throbbing at the side of her skull that was not there a moment ago. She guessed that her body was prioritizing the worst pain.

Great. The beginning of the end was starting.

Seline's screaming wasn't helping. Mila checked on Finn to distract herself from the wails, and her jaw dropped.

Finn stood in a forest of stone spikes. Each ten-foot spike had at least one Rougarou impaled on it, and several had three or more. There were also broken and torn bodies heaped around his feet, while he fought the last five of the beasts. But the most frightening thing about the whole scene was Finn himself.

He was covered from head to toe in blood and gore. It dripped from his beard and hair and made the whites of his eyes and teeth stand out all the more, giving him a crazed look. He roared like a bear and hit hard enough that the eight-foot-tall beasts were thrown back several feet and suffered broken ribs and jaws. He was like a one-man army, deep in his berserker rage and not feeling anything but the blood lust.

That wasn't to say that he hadn't sustained injury, quite the opposite. There were hundreds of claw marks across his skin, each dripping blood, some deep enough that she could see muscle and bone. Mila worried that he would die of a thousand cuts before he was able to take one of the healing potions he always carried on his person.

Something Seline was screaming caught Mila's attention, and she focused on the crazed woman.

She was now sobbing along with her screams, with her arms outstretched to the sky.

"Please, Lord! Forgive me. I can do better. I can bring you your snack. We can eat her together." She broke down and blubbered for a few seconds before her voice turned stern and she pointed accusingly at the stars. "No! You will not take me. I made you what you are. You would be nothing without me. Do you hear me? Stay away from me.

No!" she switched back to her crazed child's voice. "He's coming! Yay! He's coming, so we can all go home."

"Oh, fuck." Mila's throat suddenly went dry and she scrambled to her feet, backing away from Seline. She started looking for Azoth in the shadows.

Finn took down another Rougarou, leaving only two. He grabbed one of their arms with his prosthetic and squeezed. The magical arm had no problem applying as much pressure as he desired, and with a crunch and spurt of blood, the Rougarou's arm was crushed to a pulp in Finn's diamond fist. The second wolfman took the opportunity to charge and tackled Finn to the ground. That turned out to be a mistake when Finn hammered the artificial forearm into the beast's head, crushing its skull.

Mila turned back to Seline when she started chanting. "He's here! He's here, he's here, he's here."

A black void opened in the air above Seline's squirming form. A chill ran down Mila's spine, and something primal and old in her brain screamed for her to run. She locked her jaw, stood her ground, and prayed to anyone listening that Penny had gotten the call out in time.

Azoth's gray-robed figure stepped through the void, and it winked out behind him. He slowly surveyed the area, passing over her as if she were just another dead body, but he paused when he saw Finn fighting the last Rougarou in bloody hand to hand combat. He then lowered his head and took in the pathetic form of his naked and legless disciple.

She reached out to him from her back. "You're here! Save me from the bad lady."

Azoth was quiet, just watching the display for several seconds before his creaking, thunderous voice rasped out of his dark hood.

"Pathetic."

Seline stopped moving, a look of confusion on her face.

Azoth bent down and palmed the top of Seline's head, then lifted her into the air and spun her so she could look into his hood.

Saline held onto his hand, trying to take some of the weight of her body from her where it hung by her neck.

"No, my Lord. I have been a faithful servant," she pleaded.

"You were a tool. And now you are a broken tool. But you will not go to waste," He reassured her, placing his free palm on her chest, then pulling it away, the black wisp of her soul following after. He sucked in the tendril, then inhaled deeply, drawing it out of her as she screamed a long and wretched plea for mercy that was never coming.

Seline's screams cut off as the last of her soul was pulled free, and just like Heather, her body turned to dust and fell into a too-small pile at Azoth's feet.

Azoth finally turned his attention to Mila.

She stared into the black shadows of the hood, but even with her enhanced sight, she couldn't see anything but darkness.

"You have cost me much, little Valkyrie." He cocked his head to the side. "What do you suggest I do about that?"

"Crawl back into the latrine pit you crawled out of?" Mila said with far more confidence than she felt.

A rasping sound boomed out of Azoth's hood that made

Mila want to scratch the inside of her eardrums. With disgust, she realized it was his laugh.

"Such ferocity from one so young. I remember when you all were like that—young and stupid. It was so much easier dealing with your kind back in the good old days. Then you had to rebel. Ungrateful whelps." He considered her for a minute. "Perhaps a lesson in the old ways is just what you need." He lifted his arm palm out and pointed at Mila. "I suppose you should know what's happening since once it starts, you'll be in far too much pain to comprehend anything."

Mila glanced up over Azoth's shoulder and blinked in surprise. She narrowed her eyes, and sure enough, Penny was hovering about fifty yards up and back from the action. She pointed at the phone in her hands and gave Mila a thumbs-up.

A wash of relief filled Mila and she slumped her shoulders, sending a spike of pain up her broken arm. She sucked in a breath, but Azoth either didn't notice or didn't care.

She quickly checked her power reserves and found only a tiny bit left. It wasn't much, but it was something.

"I'm going to strip your powers an inch at a time, burning away your ability to block pain first. We wouldn't want you to miss out on all the fun, after all. After that, I shall tear your skin off, and I'll be sure to heal you as I do it. All the pain and none of the release of death you Valkyries so desire. After flaying you a few times—"

"Seriously?" Mila interrupted. "You want to play 'To the pain?' Come on, dude! How about we do something more productive with our time? Like, why don't you tell me what it is you want?"

Azoth regarded her without moving. "At first, my mission was to take the Reaper back from your thieving little band, but I modified it during my long slumber. Now I will take the Reaper, but only after I have made every last Valkyrie pay what is due me for my inconvenience."

"Let me guess; your payment is torturing us to death?" Mila held up Fragar. "You might find us harder to take than you originally planned."

"I have grown tired of our talk. You will have to find out the rest of your fate as it comes." His hand came up once again, but this time he activated his spell.

A thick black mist sprayed out of his palm, engulfing Mila.

She had known it was coming and had her shield ready, but she didn't think it would have been so soon. She was now crouched behind a rapidly dissolving shield and had nowhere to run. Glancing at the northern sky, she hoped against hope that Victoria and the others would arrive in time, but it wasn't looking good for her.

She focused every bit of power she had left into the shield, but the attack was eating the magic faster than she could put it into the construct. She realized that even if she had more power to give, she wouldn't be able to feed it in fast enough and would eventually be overrun.

The pain in her arm wasn't helping either. Every time she was jostled or moved, hot needles shot into her chest. She tried her best to block it out, but the searing pain was overwhelming.

Glancing up, she saw her shield had gained several

holes, and black mist dripped all around her, sizzling where it hit the pavement. She dug for more, but there was nothing left. She simply didn't have the power to continue feeding the shield.

The golden light of her magic began to flicker, letting in the black substance. It landed on her thigh in a long string, eating through her jeans and burning through her skin with a slow persistence that was both excruciating and infuriating.

Mila meditated through the pain as best she could, closing her eyes and slowing her breathing. It wouldn't do her any good in a second, but for the moment it helped, and that was all Mila could ask for.

One last flicker and the shield died completely. Mila was confused about why she wasn't instantly consumed and opened her eyes to see a thick wall of stone where her shield used to be. She opened her mouth but was tackled from the side by Finn.

As soon as they had cleared the area she had been kneeling in, the stone wall turned to slag and a torrent of the infernal magic blasted the pavement, melting a hole in it and catching the oil in the asphalt on fire at the edges.

Finn twisted in the air so he landed on his back, Mila on his blood-soaked chest. He slammed his hand to the pavement where it glowed with a purple light. "Get the healing potion from my holster. I saw your arm."

Walls of stone started shooting out of the ground around Azoth. They blocked his view of them and bought them a little time, but Mila knew Finn couldn't keep it up forever.

"You need it more. You're going to bleed to death at this

rate," she said frantically, opening the first pocket that usually held a potion. It was empty.

He smiled. "I knew you would say that, so I already took mine. Why do you think it took so long to get over here to help?"

She opened the second pocket, slipped the test tube full of dark red liquid into her hand, and tried to open it without spilling any.

"You hold, I uncork," Finn said, keeping his real hand on the ground and using his prosthetic to pluck the cork free.

"This is going to suck," she said before downing the whole thing.

The healing started immediately, and blessedly, it started with her burning leg. The black substance was pushed to the surface, then evaporated into black steam before the wound healed completely.

"What's the plan here, darlin'? I'm running out of stone I can pull up to make walls. There is one hell of a hole in the earth below us." Finn said, sweat making the blood caked to his forehead and cheeks thin.

"Victoria and the others should be here any minute. We just need to make him stick around long enough. There won't be a better time for them to kill him than right now. This is the weakest he's ever going to be," Mila said, biting her lip with worry.

"I trust your judgment on this one."

Just then, Mila's arm began to reset itself, and she was wracked with pain. She clutched his chest and screamed as she felt the bones slide apart, find their correct position, and reset before fusing back together, and the damage the resetting had caused began to heal as well.

She rested her forehead on his chest as she sobbed a few times, then sucked in a breath and steadied herself. The pain was gone, only the memory of it remained. She sat up, straddling Finn as he concentrated on replenishing the stone that was dissolved nearly as fast as he could summon it.

She stood, spotted Fragar lying on the ground beside them, and snatched up the weapon.

"I'm just about out of material to work with here. He'll be free in less than a minute. I can't raise any of the rock he's above for some reason. It's like he's dead spot or—"

The sound of Finn choking had Mila spinning around instantly.

Three two-inch-thick black tentacles had wrapped around Finn's wrists and neck, lifting him ten feet into the air, the bases disappearing into the solid ground.

Mila immediately chopped through one of the tentacles with Fragar. One of the runes on the blade flashed as it passed through the semi-gaseous material and left a clean cut, but before she could get to the next one, the first had regenerated.

She tried over and over, but she wasn't fast enough.

Looking up, she could see Finn's face turning dark red as the tentacle around his neck flexed and slowly worked itself tighter. She tried cutting the one around his neck, but it didn't loosen, just stopped tightening for the fraction of a second it took to regenerate.

Tears of frustration were running down her cheeks, but she kept chopping, hoping it might buy Finn another second or two. In half a minute, she was having trouble seeing the tentacle through her tears.

She looked up and saw that Finn's face had gone from dark red to an alarming purple color. He motioned with bloodshot eyes that there was something behind her. She put a hand to her mouth and coughed out a sob.

She took a second to wipe the tears and snot from her face. Taking a quick deep breath, she turned, tight-lipped anger on her face.

Azoth stood there in a casual cross-armed pose, watching her struggle to cut her lover free of his trap.

"Let him go," Mila demanded, stepping closer.

The entire area had been scoured clean by his dark magic. Not even a mound of rock remained, just burned asphalt and gravel.

"Or what? I can take whatever I want for you." He tilted his head. "Actually, this is a perfect lesson for you, watching me strangle him to death just to spite you."

"There are two kinds of captives, Azoth," Mila said coldly. "There are the docile and frightened, and then there are the fighters. I'm willing to bet you know how much a *truly* motivated fighter with *nothing* to lose is to control. You let him go, and I won't fight you. I know you're taking me and there's nothing I can do to stop you, but it's up to you how difficult I am after you have me."

Azoth tilted his head to the other side, measuring her words.

Mila glanced over his shoulder to the northern sky and saw ten distant streaks of golden light heading their way. Penny saw them too, still hovering over the battle unseen and frustrated at her impotence. As soon as she spotted the incoming Valkyries, she shot toward them, presumably to guide them directly to Mila and Finn.

The sound of Finn sucking in a breath made Mila's heart sing, but she kept it off her face. She didn't dare turn her back on the infernal creature.

"Where are you going to take me?"

He sighed. "I'm not sure yet. I was thinking of finding somewhere nice and forcing the owners to serve me. Or maybe I'll kill them. Why does it matter?"

"I suppose it doesn't," Mila agreed.

"Come, pet. I grow bored here. We leave. Now." He pointed to the ground beside him as if he expected her to heel like a dog.

Mila glanced over his shoulder again and saw that the Valkyries were about halfway there. She needed to stall for longer.

"What guarantee do I have that you won't come after him once you have me?" Mila asked, trying for as much time as possible.

Azoth gave his mind-numbing laugh, raking at Mila's ears. "What guarantee do I have that you will remain cooperative once I have you?"

Mila frowned. That was answered by her being his captive and him being free. It was a fairly simple logic problem. The jailer had infinite opportunities to exact revenge for the prisoner's disobedience. In contrast, the prisoner only had their agreement and only one opportunity to exact their revenge, but it would be too late by then.

Mila thought back to Azoth's plans thus far, and she had to admit that they weren't very good. Why set up near a town, steal a significant number of locals, and then stick around waiting for people to find you?

Even then, she didn't understand how he didn't deduce she was stalling for time.

He was powerful and cruel beyond measure, but he was kind of stupid.

That was how she needed to fight this thing. Not like a berserker. She needed to fight like a shield maiden.

"I'll make you deal that will make your life much easier. A kind of guarantee," Mila said, waiting for his answer.

He tilted his head again. "Very well. What is it?"

"Give me five minutes with my lover back there to say goodbye, and I'll let you use one of those antimagic collars you had on Heather on me when we travel. That way, there is no way I could ever escape you."

She swallowed, hoping he didn't see through that load of goblin shit. While he considered, she glanced over his shoulder again, and nearly shouted for joy. They were closing fast. Less than twenty se—

"Why do you keep looking past me? It's rude not to make eye contact with your master." He looked over his shoulder, the ten incoming Valkyrie as plain as day.

He slowly turned back toward her, but she had backed up several steps when he turned. She knew he would make a lunge for her if he thought he could catch her quickly.

The darkness in the hood somehow grew darker as his anger boiled over.

"You Valkyries think you're so clever. Always laying traps for the Drudes, but a Drude is a slippery prize to hold for long." He waved a hand, and a black void opened behind him. "I'll be back for you. I wish to peel your skin.

We shall have a grand time, you and I. Before I eat you, that is."

He stepped back into the void, and it vanished as ten women slammed into the ground, riding inside what looked like lightning.

Mila didn't give her ten sisters a second look. Instead, she spun on her heel and ran to Finn.

CHAPTER TWENTY-EIGHT

The tentacles had vanished along with Azoth and dropped Finn ten feet to the ground.

He was sitting up and still covered in blood, taking deep, even breaths, but he was the most beautiful thing she had ever seen.

She fell into his lap, wrapping her arms around his neck and pulling him in for a kiss.

Penny landing in her lap a minute later was the only reason she stopped kissing him.

Mila turned to her friend. "What?"

Penny hiked a thumb sideways, and Mila followed the thumb to Victoria, who was dressed in full combat armor, her longsword on her back. She was staring down at Mila with a disapproving look. Beside her was a young, for lack of a better term, goth valley girl.

Mila climbed awkwardly off Finn's lap and helped him to his feet, Penny climbing to his shoulder and perching with an arm on his blood-soaked hair.

"I'm going to go see if we can salvage the Death Machine. It looks like you have business to take care of." Finn nodded toward the two women.

Mila nodded. "I'll just be a minute."

He squeezed her hand, then walked down the ruined road to where he had last seen the bike.

Mila watched him go until it became awkward and then turned to the two women. She held out a blood-covered hand to the goth girl. "I'm Mila Winters."

"Oh, I know who you are." She took the offered hand without hesitation, not seeming to notice the blood. "I'm Missy Walker, the eldest. I have to say I'm very impressed with your work here. If we had been here ten seconds earlier, we would have had him."

Mila didn't know if she liked the nonchalant attitude surrounding letting a mass-murdering psycho get away, but nodded to keep the peace for now. "It was a close thing."

"We can only stay for a few minutes. Your drain on us is quite strong," Missy said, tossing a blue pigtail over her shoulder. "Speaking of, how have you grown in power so fast? It usually takes us a lifetime or two to fully understand our conviction."

Mila smiled and looked over her shoulder at Finn, who was pulling the wrecked bike from where it had been wedged under the guard rail.

"Finn showed me the way. He's surprisingly wise," Mila said with a smile.

"I had heard you were a champion of a hero, but I have to say, no one mentioned he was a dwarf. And a royal if those magical tattoos are any indication. You really weren't messing around choosing him, were you?"

"Oh, I didn't pick him," Mila said, holding her hands up. "He picked me. Walked up to me sure as can be with a fucking dragon on his shoulder. It was pretty much history from there."

Missy gave Mila with an appraising look that far outpaced her body's experience. It was the look of what most people would call an old soul, and in Missy's case, it was true.

"I'm glad to have some fresh blood. Should spice things up," Missy said, looking down the road to where Penny was using the repair spell she had learned from Howard to fix the damage to the bike. Finn was freaking out with excitement. "Be sure to watch out for that one. He's unique to *Earth*."

Mila nodded. "Penny, Finn, and I are all unique. We're a funny little family, but it *is* a family. *We look out for each other.*"

The Valkyries bid them farewell and took off, with promises of speaking by phone that Friday.

Penny was able to repair the bike completely, along with cleaning and mending their clothes, one of her handier spells.

Finn dropped a note to Hermin and Garret that there was a cleanup on the mountain road that they would need to take care of. The two Huldus grumbled, but they knew things like that were bound to happen when evil needed to be stopped.

Despite the fight and wreck, they were still on time to

meet Danica and Phil at the Refinery. They ate and drank and sang karaoke until Mila and Finn were little better than zombies from exhaustion.

Penny walked home with Mila and Finn, who strolled hand in hand the block and a half home. Once inside, Penny went to her room, claiming she needed to arrange her new starter hoard, bidding them good night before disappearing.

Mila and Finn stumbled into their room, stripped naked at the foot of the bed, then fell asleep within a minute of covering up.

Mila was having one of those rare dreams where she knew it was a dream but was able to stay in it. She didn't seem to have any control of the dream, but she was able to move about freely.

She found herself in an open-air market in what she assumed was a Middle Eastern country, but she had never seen a place like it in real life and was amazed at the detail in the dream, from the languages to the small trinkets for sale at the stalls.

She browsed the shops and vendors, but quickly grew bored and wondered when she was going to wake up.

She found a large fountain at the center of the market and sat on the edge, crossing her ankles and swishing a hand through the cool, clean water.

She was starting to think she should start doing crazy things to make herself wake up, like jump off a building or something, when she saw a robed figure passing through the market.

Robed men and women weren't unusual in the market. They were everywhere, but she recognized that robe. It was Azoth's.

Not liking where this was going, she still decided to follow him. After all, it was her dream; it wasn't like he could hurt her here.

She kept her distance but always had eyes on the back of his gray head. He led her deeper into the city, where there were fewer people, but still enough to hide among them if he turned around, which he never did.

The crowd on the streets thinned, then they became abandoned as they entered a bombed-out section of the city. Mila started hiding at corners and only following after Azoth turned, which he did quite often as if zigzagging his way across the city.

She watched him traveling down an abandoned street with three burned-out cars still in their parking spaces. This time, instead of turning down a main street, he turned down an alley.

Mila jogged to the alley's entrance, hearing clear signs of a struggle. Mila glanced around the corner and saw Azoth, his back to her, watching a woman quickly and efficiently take out five attackers with a combination of martial arts and spell-slinging.

The woman's spells were particularly vicious in Mila's opinion. For example, she removed one attacker's legs with a spell, but instead of using an explosive of some sort or a wind blade, she shot what looked like a bike chain from a bubble. The chain wrapped around the attacker's leg and proceeded to saw it off as the chain spun and tightened slowly. The attacker had been screaming in pain the entire fight until she crushed his head with a cinderblock.

Azoth began to clap as if he had just seen a great theater performance. "Wonderful, but I can help you become better."

"Fuck off, old man," the woman said, going through her attackers' pockets for cash or coin. Mila was starting to think this wasn't as straightforward as she had first believed.

Azoth continued walking toward her, but either she didn't notice or didn't think he was a threat. He walked up behind her, standing so close that if he lifted his foot, it would hit her squatting ass.

She stood and rounded on him, her mouth opening to yell something when her eyes widened in confusion.

Azoth slapped a palm to her chest, then pulled it back, revealing the thread of her soul. He began to pull it out like Mila had seen him do twice now, and felt sorrow for the woman.

Then something different happened, and Mila was fascinated.

Azoth pressed his other palm to the woman's chest, but this time when he pulled the hand away, there was a black thread that led from him into her. He slowly exchanged part of her soul for an equal amount of his.

The process took forever, but when it was done, there was a maniacal glint in the woman's eye that hadn't been there before.

"Master." The woman bowed to him.

Azoth turned, and Mila found that she could no longer move. His dark hood regarded her, and she got the feeling he was smiling.

"I haven't forgotten about you, Mila." His creaking voice made her cringe. "I will gather my people, then we shall come, and I will take you to be my personal pet. I can't wait for all the fun we'll have. See you soon."

Mila awoke with a start and scrambled away from Finn's sleeping chest, gasping and looking around the room for enemies.

Finn was on his feet in a flash, brandishing the baseball bat they kept beside the bed. "What is it? Did someone get in?" He saw that Mila was holding her head in her hands.

He approached her, gently putting a hand on her bare shoulder. "Darlin', what happened?"

She lifted her head from her hands, her face a mask of rage. She was so angry that her shoulders shook uncontrollably.

"That motherfucking coward just made his first mistake is what happened."

The End

Mila won the first round, but the Druid is waking up. His powers of infernal magic can use nightmares to drive people insane or exchange bits of their soul for infernal magic and infect them to be his thralls. Will a Lone Valkyrie be enough of a match? How long can a goblin hold its breath? Read *Choose the Slain* to find out if Mila can master celestial magic and help save her kind.

Get sneak peeks, exclusive giveaways, behind the scenes content, and more.
PLUS you'll be notified of special **one day only fan pricing** on new releases.

Sign up today to get free stories.

CLICK HERE

or visit: https://marthacarr.com/read-free-stories/

Thanks for reading the first book in the Lone Valkyrie series. If you're new to the Terranavis universe then welcome! You may have guessed that this series is a "continuation" of another series, and I recommend you check that out. It's called <u>The Adventures of Finnegan Dragonbender</u>, and fills in a lot of those tiny details you may be curious about. That being said, it is by no means required reading to enjoy this series.

For of those of you that have come from the Adventures of Finnegan Dragonbender, welcome back! It's so good to have you back.

So, over the last couple of months one of my cats, Bub, has become quite the cry baby. He will come into my office and yell at me for hours if I don't pay attention to him... literally hours. I timed it once; he never gave up.

Even now he is laying on my desk, his chest and front paws draped over one of my forearms while I'm typing this, and generally making a nuisance of himself. It's really annoying, and only slightly endearing.

It's annoying and disruptive and pain in the ass. I just want him to give me some space, and shut the hell up, so I can work!

Me and my wife recently moved to a new city, and my writing has started to take off.(I know this seems like a completely random direction to take after a short story about my cat, but hang in there)

My wife is a smarty-pants and has a good job where people call her by her earned degree. You know, a profession. She has an office with windows, and her name on the door and everything. There are even people that come to her for answers because she's the only one in the state who can answer them. (I realize I married up. In fact, the only thing I question about her judgment is the fact that she chose to end up with me.)

While at work she is constantly interacting with people; on the phone, people in her office, out in the field, etc. She gets more social interaction that she can handle by the end of every day.

Me, on the other hand? I work from home. My office mates are the cats. Let's just say that I don't exactly have meaningful conversation for a good nine hours out of the day. By the time my wife gets home I'm half mad from talking to myself. I haven't seen another human since she left that morning.

We eat dinner. Watch some TV. Talk about her work. Talk about my work.

Then at around 8pm she goes and reads a book, or putters around on Facebook or what have you, and I go into my office and watch YouTube, or play a video game. At 10:30 or so we go to bed and do it all again.

This is the compromise we both came to after a particular incident that changed my view of how things work completely.

Back when we had first moved to our new house and I was working full time from home, my wife came home and I was stir crazy. I started talking her ear off, and sitting really close to her on the couch.

I was excited she was home and I finally had someone to talk to that could talk back.

She was exhausted from too much human interaction.

It did not go well.

The straw that broke the camel's back came when she was sitting on the couch, trying to read a book, and I laid down and put my head in her lap.

She exploded.

She told me she just needed to decompress from work. I countered that I hadn't talked out loud in 8 hours and needed some human time.

Immediately we realized we hadn't been communicating very well, and so we talked about what would work. So now I get my human interaction, and she gets her decompression time.

Earlier today I was trying to write and Bub jumped up on my desk plopping down on my arm and started purring. I almost shooed him away, angry that he interrupted me again.

Instead I started laughing.

I got it. I was my wife's Bub. Always in her business, and never giving her a moments peace.

I picked Bub up and laid him on the floor, then proceeded to pet the ever living shit out of him. He was in heaven. Drooling and purring like it was the best thing in the world. I did that for a good five minutes until he suddenly jumped up and ran into the other room. He had had enough.

I had a good five hours peace before he came back.

Sometimes we have to give a little to get a little. In fact, I'll go as far as, we *always* have to give a little to get a little.

Peace fellow humans. I hope we all can find the balance in life.

Charley Case
(Boise, Id)

Okay, make sure you read the hobbies question – Metal detecting! Knife throwing! You never know what lurks in the heart of your graphic designer. Kayla is one of the prime examples of why it's a blast working with LMBPN. A great graphics designer at my disposal! She's creative and always coming up with a better twist for what we need. That's the best kind of artist. The kind who takes my pile of ideas and adds in their own flare to create something eye-catching and original.

Writing a good book with a great cover and a snappy blurb are just the start. Hello Marketing… That's where Kayla comes swooping in with graphics to grab a reader's attention long enough to take a look at that cover and a few words about the book. Or build a web site – Kayla totally redid mine at www.marthacarr.com – or a Facebook banner or create a new mug. The list goes on and on and on.

And because Kayla is available to take care of that part of the picture, I can get back to writing. It all works out.

Martha Carr

1. Tell our readers a bit about yourself.

I'm a graphic and web designer living in Nebraska with my husband and two sons. I also like to write, but I've put away my author hat for now to focus on graphic design. I love acquiring new skills and I love working with other creatives.

2. Tell us a little bit about your history with writing.

I published my first novel in 2012 with a small press. It was the first book in my paranormal romance series and I've published a total of four novels. I have a few things in the works, including a large epic fantasy series, but I'm just casually writing for now with no plans to publish quite yet.

3. What genre(s) do you write?

I write paranormal romance, urban fantasy, epic fantasy, and I also dabble in other genres when inspiration strikes.

4. What genre(s) do you read?

I read just about everything. Currently, I'm really going back to my epic fantasy roots. However, I've got horror, science fiction, urban fantasy, paranormal romance, mysteries, thrillers, and more on my bookshelf and in my kindle library.

5. Do you have hobbies?

I have too many hobbies...more than any person could possibly need. I like writing, drawing, painting, crafts, metal detecting, sewing, scrapbooking, jewelry making, and even knife throwing just to name a few.

6. What is one of your goals for the new year?

My goal for 2020 is to improve my graphic design craft and to improve my writing craft. I've been working at both for quite a while and I'm always learning new techniques that allow me to take my art to the next level.

7. Do you have a website you want to share?

My author site is under construction until I publish again, but my graphic design site is currygraphicdesign.com.

If smart phones and GPS rule the world - why am I hunting a magic compass to save the planet?

Austin Detective Maggie Parker has seen some weird things in her day, but finding a surly gnome rooting through her garage beats all.

Her world is about to be turned upside down in a frantic search for 4 Elementals.

Each one has an artifact that can keep the Earth humming along, but they need her to unite them first.

Unless the forces against her get there first.

AVAILABLE ON AMAZON AND IN KINDLE UNLIMITED!

OTHER BOOKS IN THE TERRANAVIS
UNIVERSE

The Adventures of Maggie Parker Series

The Witches of Pressler Street

Other books by Martha Carr

Other books by Charley Case

**JOIN THE TERRANAVIS UNIVERSE FACEBOOK
GROUP**

FOLLOW TERRANAVIS UNIVERSE ON FACEBOOK

OTHER LMBPN PUBLISHING BOOKS

To be notified of new releases and special promotions from
LMBPN publishing, please join our email list:

http://lmbpn.com/email/

For a complete list of books published by LMBPN please visit the
following pages:

https://lmbpn.com/books-by-lmbpn-publishing/

All LMBPN Audiobooks are Available at Audible.com and
iTunes. For a complete list of audiobooks visit:

www.lmbpn.com/audible

CONNECT WITH THE AUTHORS

Martha Carr Social

Website:
http://www.marthacarr.com

Facebook:
https://www.facebook.com/groups/MarthaCarrFans/

https://www.facebook.com/terranavisuniverse/

Michael Anderle Social

Michael Anderle Social
Website:
http://www.lmbpn.com

Email List:
http://lmbpn.com/email/

Facebook
https://www.facebook.com/TheKurtherianGambitBooks/